OPHELIA RED

A. S. FRENCH

NEONOIR BOOKS

Science Fiction

The Time Traveller's Murder

The Mercy Sleep

Bodies

The Arcane Supernatural Thriller Series

Book one: The Arcane

Book two: The Arcane Identity

Book three: The Arcane Quest

Book four: The Arcane Ultimatum

The Ella Finn Fantasy Novella Series

Ella and the Elementals

Ella and the Multiverse

Ella and the Monsters

Ella and the Dreamers

Supernatural Short Stories

Dead Souls

The Shadow

Go to www.andrewsfrench.com for more information.

1 SHE'S IN PARTIES

The smell of rosebushes filled the air. Ophelia Red, a bee in one hand and a Coke in the other, marched through the garden. The revellers parted before her as they glanced at Ophelia's ruby hair and the insect sitting in her palm. The bee tickled her skin as she put it down, pouring Coke on her finger and offering it to the distressed creature. The bee devoured it in a heartbeat.

'You'll kill it like that.'

She peered at the man in swimming trunks staring at her. A lion tattoo covered his chest as the sunlight reflected off his gold tooth. She couldn't see the skin on his arms or legs, only tattoos of mythical creatures: dragons, unicorns and elves.

'What?' she said.

He shook his head, sending dandruff into the roses.

'You want a solution of sugar and water to restore an exhausted bee, and only offer it white granulated sugar. Any artificial or diet sweeteners can harm them, and that Coke will kill it.'

As he spoke, the bee fluttered into life and flew away.

Ophelia grinned at the illustrated man. 'It was that or a shot of vodka, and we don't want a drunken bee terrorising the guests at this shindig, do we?'

He came at her like a vulture at a corpse, smelling of sweat and cheap cologne.

'Did you know the first Coke drink was red wine mixed with cocaine, advertised as a brain tonic to relieve headaches and exhaustion?'

She didn't encourage him with a reply, knowing it would have been like buying Jeffrey Dahmer a second fridge. Instead, she returned to the kitchen and grabbed a bottle of Mexican lager. From the living room, Madonna was singing *Like A Virgin*. Ophelia took a long swig and buried the memories of her father's alcoholism behind those of her mother's indifference.

'I bet there's few of them here.' She turned to see a purple-haired woman grinning at her. 'Virgins, I mean.'

The alcohol warmed Ophelia's mouth. 'Is this a sex party?'

The newcomer spat vodka over the floor. 'Good God, I hope not.' She glanced into the living room before peering through the window into the garden. 'Have you seen the state of the men here?'

Ophelia slurped her drink. 'I don't know anyone here. I'm a gate crasher.'

The purple-haired woman didn't seem to care.

'My boss asked me to come with him. He feels it's easier to meet women if you're already with one. Like being married is attractive to women, you know?' Ophelia didn't know. 'He thinks it proves something about him if at least one woman already deems him dateable.'

'What do you do?' Ophelia said.

'My name's Chloe and I'm a funeral director.'

That's appropriate.

'You must have some tales to tell.'

She grabbed Ophelia and pulled her towards the window.

'You don't know the half of it.' She pointed at the clown in the garden entertaining the guests. 'Do you see that bloke?'

'Ronald McDonald?'

Chloe narrowed her eyes in confusion. 'No, that comedian over there. We had a dead clown at the funeral parlour once, buried in a full costume with makeup. The whole family was clowns, and all the friends were clowns. And at the family's request, the funeral directors were clowns too. They supplied costumes and did our makeup. Family and friends had one tear drop painted near the eye.'

Ophelia sipped on the drink, her interest now awakened. 'Doesn't it bother you, staring into so many dead faces?'

It had never bothered her, but she was curious how others felt.

Chloe's face brightened. 'No, never. The eyes usually flatten after death like an old grape. They do, however, remain with the body. We don't remove them. Instead, you can use an eye cap to put over the flattened eyeball to recreate the natural curvature. You can inject tissue builder directly into the eyeball and fill it up. And sometimes, the embalming fluid will fill the eye to normal size.'

'It sounds fascinating.'

Chloe beamed. 'Well, I think so, but most people don't.' She leant closer so Ophelia could smell the lavender in her hair. 'Many people don't understand. I've lost several boyfriends because of it and my mother thinks I'm a vampire.'

'At least the customers don't talk back to you.'

Chloe snorted like an asthmatic hyena. 'That's true.'

'What made you go into that line of work?'

'Childhood trauma.' She laughed again. 'No, not really. When I was ten, there was a terrible collision near my house, and a man in a truck didn't make it. When the coroner arrived, my family and I stood around with the neighbours. He pronounced him deceased. Then they put him on a stretcher and his head turned to the side, looking straight at me. I remember being curious about what happens to the human body when people die.'

Ophelia knew what she meant. She was twelve years old when she realised something was different with her, sitting cross-legged and ankle-deep in blood that wasn't hers, reciting the alphabet backwards.

'Are you still curious?'

Chloe nodded. 'The human brain is fascinating, especially when you hold one in your hands.' She inched closer to Ophelia. 'But that's enough about me. So what do you do, mysterious party crasher?'

Ophelia should have told her something mundane, a fictitious job that wouldn't leave any lasting memories for when the police arrived. But the boredom had got the better of her, and now she wanted some fun.

And maybe she'd drunk too much.

'I'm an online dating ghost-writer.'

Confusion crept across Chloe's face. 'You set up dates for ghosts?'

Ophelia laughed. 'No. I write profiles for online dating sites for those who struggle to produce their own.'

'Wow,' Chloe said. 'Isn't that like lying?'

'Of course not. I'm cupid with a computer, that's all.'

Chloe pointed out of the window. 'Maybe you could

write one for that loser.' Ophelia peered at the tattooed man standing on his hands. 'Duff by name and by nature.'

'That's Larry Duff?'

'Yes. Do you know him?'

Ophelia shook her head. 'I overheard somebody talking about him. Isn't this his house?' Now she had confirmation on the target.

Chloe frowned. 'It's his celebration. This is in poor taste if you ask me.'

'Why?'

Chloe lowered her voice. 'He hit a ten-year-old girl with his car, killing her. You'd think he'd go to prison for that, wouldn't you?' Ophelia nodded. 'All he got was a six-month driving ban and points on his licence. It's scandalous.'

Ophelia agreed. 'The girl's family must be devastated.'

'Oh, it got even worse for them. The father jumped off a bridge not long after his daughter's death, and from what I've heard, the mother is now sucking on sleeping tablets as if they're sweets. She can't pay the mortgage on the house, so she'll also lose that.' She nodded at Duff amusing his guests. 'And all because that moron was on his phone while driving.'

'Did he tell the police that?'

Chloe whispered, 'Nope. Only his friends know about it.'

Ophelia peered at the illustrated man, now knowing why somebody had hired her to kill him. She rarely knew the reasons for her contracts, but she only had two rules: no kids and nothing within thirty miles of her home. Two days ago, she'd arrived in Leeds – seventy-five miles from her place in Redcar – spending the first day scouting the area around Duff's house. So when she'd turned up in the street this afternoon, it had been a pleasant surprise to see the celebrations, surveying the premises as she hid in plain sight amongst revellers.

She hadn't planned to kill Duff there and then, but she had the means in her bag if she had the right opening: fast and slow-acting poisons; two syringes; a small knife; and a garrotte. Ophelia thought about those tools as she heard *Dancing Queen* blasting through the house. She left Chloe in the kitchen and returned to the garden, watching as Duff hugged a clown. She sat in a chair near the roses, reaching into her jacket to remove one of her phones. She pushed her thumb into the screen to unlock it and opened the app for her Cayman Islands bank account, smiling when she saw the deposit for half of her payment. Then she returned the phone to her pocket. Now it was a waiting game.

OPHELIA STAYED INSIDE until ten o'clock, watching everybody leave apart from her and four others. Before exiting the front door, she checked the garden and every room. Then she went across the road and waited some more. By midnight, everyone but Duff had left the building. She gave it another twenty minutes before moving to the rear of the house and the garden, gripping the key she'd taken earlier. She let herself in and peered into her bag, unsure what to use to kill him. She moved into the living room and considered the options, finding him slumped on the sofa. He was drunk and out cold.

Time for an old favourite.

She returned to the kitchen for a tea towel. She had to place the cloth over his mouth, her knee on his stomach, and nature and the alcohol would do the rest. The pressure would induce him to vomit, and since it wouldn't have anywhere to go because of the towel, he'd choke. Ophelia was moving towards him when she heard the front door open.

Shit!

She hurried into the far corner behind a large bookshelf.

Maybe I should sit on the sofa and pretend I'm drunk from the party.

Before she could do anything, a blonde woman entered the room, pointing a gun at the sleeping Larry Duff.

Her hand trembled as she spoke. 'This is for killing my daughter, you piece of shit.'

Daughter? The girl he'd killed – this was the mother?

Ophelia could let her shoot him and still get paid.

But if she's here to kill him, she can't have been the one who hired me.

The woman was caressing the trigger as Ophelia stepped out of the shadows.

'You don't need to do that.'

She jerked her head towards Ophelia, swinging the pistol around.

'What... what did you say?'

Ophelia kept a careful eye on that weapon. 'What's your daughter's name?'

A single tear dripped onto the woman's cheek. 'Laura. Her name was Laura.' She glanced at Duff. 'And this piece of shit killed her. The law did nothing, and he's here partying like a fucking rock star.'

'How did you get into the house?'

'The front door was unlocked.'

Great. I should have checked that.

She stepped closer to Ophelia. 'Are you his girlfriend?'

Ophelia shook her head. 'No. I'm here to kill him.'

The woman's eyes glazed over. 'Why? Did he hurt you as well?'

'Does it matter why? You can leave and I'll ensure he gets what's coming to him.'

She waved the gun at Ophelia. 'It matters to me. And why should I believe you? You could be his partner and a lying scumbag like he is.'

'Do you want to watch me do it?'

The woman thought about it for ten seconds. 'Yes.'

Ophelia moved towards Duff, watching his chest move up and down as the drool slipped between his lips. The lion tattoo glared at her, growling as Duff's ribs vibrated. She climbed onto the sofa, her legs on either side of him, glancing at the distraught mother.

'What's your name?'

'Katrina,' she said.

'Last chance to leave, Katrina.'

She shook her head and the gun. 'No. I need to see this.'

Ophelia placed the material over his face, and then put her knee on his stomach. After thirty seconds, his eyes flicked open in panic. She bathed in his fear as he tried to fight her, but he was out of luck. It took four minutes before he stopped struggling and she got off him, hanging onto the vomit-stained cloth.

Katrina walked to him, gazing into the dead face of the man who'd killed her daughter. 'What do we do now?'

Ophelia took the gun from her, putting it into her pocket along with the cloth.

'Did you drive here?'

Katrina nodded. 'Yes, but I didn't park near the house. It's a ten-minute walk from here.'

Ophelia grabbed her arm and pulled her into the kitchen.

'We're leaving through the back. Stick to the shadows and twenty yards in front of me, and head straight for the car.'

Katrina didn't argue. Ophelia followed her into the street.

Now, what do I do with her?

2 BACK TO THE OLD HOUSE

'You smell of vomit,' Katrina said.

They were sitting in her car, and Ophelia thought the grieving mother might be about to throw up.

'Do you have alcohol at home?'

Katrina nodded. 'Plenty.'

Ophelia fastened the seatbelt. 'Okay. Take us there. We've got a lot to talk about.'

THIRTY MINUTES LATER, she sat in the living room, sipping on a gin and tonic. They'd taken a detour to dispose of the gun and the vomit cloth in the river. Now Katrina slumped on the sofa opposite her.

'Why did you kill Duff?'

Ophelia chewed on a piece of ice. 'Somebody paid me.'

Katrina's eyes bulged. 'Who would do that?'

Ophelia shrugged. 'I thought it might be you.'

'Me?' Katrina laughed. 'I can barely pay for food. How much does a murder cost?'

'It varies. Duff was worth fifty grand to someone.'

Katrina grabbed at her throat before she choked on her whisky.

'Fifty grand! Jesus.'

Ophelia swallowed the ice. 'It's a decent living.'

'Do you normally leave witnesses?'

The cube chilled her mouth. 'No.'

'So you brought me here to kill me?'

'I'm not sure what I'll do with you.' Ophelia glanced around the living room, seeing toys and children's books everywhere. 'Do you have any suggestions?'

Katrina's face darkened. Reaching for the bottle on the table next to her, she held it so Ophelia could see the contents: sleeping pills.

'You'll be quicker than these, and do me a favour.' Her eyelids trembled like butterfly wings on fast forward. 'I can't pay you, but I don't want the vomit thing either. Do you have a quick and painless option?'

A chill ran through Ophelia's fingers. 'What do you do for a living?'

Katrina returned the pills to the table. 'I trained as a computer programmer at university. That's where I met Brian. Now, I'm a forensic computer analyst. My husband and I worked for the same company before things got complicated.'

Ophelia scrutinised her, understanding she wasn't talking about her daughter's death.

'What happened?'

'It wasn't computers that brought Brian and me together, but our love of gambling. It started at university. They had several quiz machines in the bar, and we'd spend hours on them. Unfortunately, it didn't help with either of our student debts. By the time we got our degrees, we owed over a hundred grand between us.'

'How long ago was this?'

'Ten years. I was pregnant with Laura. Once we left university, we lived with his parents before finding jobs for the same company. His mother hated me, but I put up with it. Then we married, bought a house, and had a lovely baby girl to fawn over.'

'Had you started paying your debt?'

'Hardly. What we owed never seemed to reduce, with the mortgage payments, childcare expenses, and everyday bills.'

'But you had well-paid jobs?'

'Until six months ago, just before Laura's death.'

'You were both still betting?'

Katrina removed a phone from her pocket and placed it on her leg.

'Do you know how easy it is to place a bet online?' Ophelia shook her head. 'Gambling is like having a frontal lobotomy. You sit there and listen to the music, which relaxes you and makes you feel better.' She waved the mobile at Ophelia. 'And when it's all done electronically, so you don't even have the money in your hand, it's like living in a fairy tale. All of it is unreal, and you have flashing lights and music attacking your senses. So it doesn't matter what you lose because none of it is real.'

'How much do you and your husband owe?'

'Including our student debts, about a hundred grand. And we're six months behind on the mortgage for this house. We talked about going to a loan shark, but...'

'You stole from your company instead?'

'It was easier that way. We both had access to the finances through the computer system.' She lowered her head. 'But we weren't very good at covering our tracks. Our employer discovered what we'd done less than a week into our criminal careers. We were both sacked on the spot. I thought that was the worst thing that could happen to me, but it wasn't.' She raised her eyes to stare at Ophelia. 'A few days later, Duff hits Laura with his car. And then Brian jumps off a bridge.' She finished her drink. 'So here we are, and you're about to do me a favour.'

Ophelia cradled the glass in her hands. 'Perhaps.'

'How did you become an assassin for hire?'

'It's a long story.'

'I've got plenty of time. Or have I?' Her laugh rattled the top of the table between them. 'How do your clients contact you?'

'Through the dark web.'

Katrina put her drink down. 'But how do you know you can trust them?'

Ophelia relaxed on the sofa.

Why am I talking to her like this? Is it because I'm going to kill her, anyway?

I can't leave any witnesses.

And this woman wants to die – she's got nothing left to live for.

'They pay half the fee upfront, the minimum being twenty-five thousand non- refundable. So nobody is going to throw that amount away on a whim.'

'Yes, but what if it's the police or somebody else trying to trap you?'

Ophelia shrugged. 'That's one of the risks you take in this business. Once I've received the payment and the details, I check the target to ensure the contract is legit.'

'And that's what you did with Duff?'

'Yes.'

'And you thought it was me who'd hired you?'

'I didn't know and didn't care. I don't look to see who is hiring me or ask why. I just do the job.'

'What if you feel uneasy about the contract? Say if it's an innocent person or a child?'

'I don't kill children, and nobody is innocent.'

'What if a client pays you to kill someone doing good in the world?'

'I don't make moral judgements.'

Katrina laughed. 'Maybe you could teach me how to do it. I could pay my debts then.'

'You believe you're capable of killing a person?'

'Yes. I would have killed Duff.'

'You had good reason for that. But think about those innocent people you asked me about. Could you kill one of them?'

Katrina grabbed her empty glass and stood. 'While I muse on that, would you like another drink?'

Ophelia got up. 'Sure, but I need the bathroom first.'

'Top of the stairs, second on your left.'

She headed for the kitchen while Ophelia went to the toilet. Once Ophelia had finished, she checked the bedrooms, stepping into one that must have been Laura's: everything was purple, including the wallpaper and the sheets. She glanced at the computer desk and the full bookcase, recognising novels she'd loved as a kid: the *His Dark Materials* trilogy; *The Dark is Rising*; *Earthsea*; and *The Arcane* series. She peered at the covers and remembered the collection of books and comics she'd had as a teenager. They'd been her only friends until the day her mother had tossed them away.

'You're too old for childish things,' her mother had said

as she ripped out the pages of eight-year-old Ophelia's cherished copy of *The Golden Compass*.

But that was long ago, and Ophelia had a different name then. She pushed the memory back into the shadows and wondered what to do with the woman downstairs.

Katrina has nothing to live for, so I'll be doing her a favour.

As she considered that, she heard glass breaking below. She left Laura's bedroom and returned to the living room.

Only to find a masked man with a large knife placed against Katrina's neck.

'Which one of you is Rossetti?' he said.

Ophelia scanned the room, checking for other intruders, unsurprised that he knew her secret name.

'Are you from Hitsville?'

He pushed the blade closer to Katrina's flesh. 'I guess it's you, then. Get on your knees and put your hands behind you.'

She shook her head. 'No.'

'Do it,' he growled. 'Or I'll slit her throat.'

Ophelia laughed. 'I don't care. She means nothing to me.' She stepped towards him. 'What's your name in Hitsville?'

He moved back and pushed up against the sofa with Katrina against him.

'I'm not telling you that. Now get on your knees.'

Ophelia gazed into Katrina's eyes. Then she nodded to the grieving mother. Katrina grinned as she stamped on her assailant's foot. He screamed as she wriggled from his grasp, the knife brushing against her throat and drawing blood. She fell forward and Ophelia grabbed her, the two women stumbling back as the masked man jumped on one leg. When he lowered the blade, Ophelia pounced.

She threw herself into him, taking them over the sofa and into a table. Photos of Laura and Katrina shattered on the floor, showering glass and cutting her fingers. She grabbed for the knife with her other hand, clawing at his wrist as he tried to push her away.

But she failed, and he dropped the blade.

He got both hands around her neck and squeezed.

Ophelia's breath fizzed from her as she clutched at his arms. They were stuck in the space between the back of the sofa and the wall, her body twitching as his nails dug into her skin. She pulled at his clothes, trying to drag him away. Ophelia peered into the eyes behind the mask, hearing him grunt as he squeezed harder.

Her eyelids flickered, and her vision blurred as a porcelain figure of a pig crashed into his head. It split into pieces, raining blood everywhere, forcing him to let go of her and jerk towards his attacker.

It was the opportunity Ophelia needed.

As she coughed, she raised her arm and punched him in the gut. Then she grabbed his waist and threw him into the wall, so he hit it head first. She wiped her throat and staggered towards him, unable to stop Katrina from plunging the knife into his chest. He groaned as he clutched at the blade, slipping down onto the carpet.

Ophelia rested against the sofa and watched the blood seep through his clothes. Then she removed his mask.

'Do you recognise him?' Katrina said.

'Nope.' Ophelia gazed at the dying man. 'What's your Hitsville name?'

Blood dripped over his lips. 'Darknight64,' he spluttered.

'Did you follow us from Duff's house?'

The word crawled out of his mouth. 'Yes.'

'How much did they pay you for me?'

'A lot.'

Then he died.

Ophelia turned from him. She went to the kitchen and poured a gin and tonic. When she returned to the living room, Katrina was on the sofa, supping straight from the whisky bottle and rubbing at the wound on her neck. Ophelia sat opposite her.

'What's Hitsville?' Katrina said.

The liquid scratched at Ophelia's throat. 'It's the corner of the dark web where assassins ply their trade.'

'And you're Rossetti?'

'You can call me Ophelia.'

'Okay. Why would another assassin try to kill you?'

'I don't know, but he followed us from Duff's place without knowing which of us was the target.'

'But he would have killed us both?'

'Yes. You can't leave witnesses.' She stared at Katrina. 'But he had to make sure before doing the deed.' She smiled at her. 'Do you still want to kill people for money?'

Katrina glanced at the corpse in the corner. 'Well, I've already started with a freebie.'

Ophelia finished her drink. 'Indeed.'

'What do we do now?'

'We?' Ophelia stood. 'I don't have to do anything. You're the one with the dead man in your house.'

She went to the body, checking for anything that might illuminate the situation. Katrina followed her.

'You're going to leave me like this after I saved your life?'

Ophelia found nothing on the man. 'I had everything under control before you interfered.'

Katrina laughed. 'You were lulling him in by letting him strangle you, then?'

Ophelia glanced at the damage in the room before returning her gaze to the woman who'd killed the mysterious assassin.

What am I going to do now?

3 DRIVE, SHE SAID

They wrapped the body in a tarpaulin from the garage and dumped it in the boot of the car.

Katrina lit a cigarette. 'What do we do next?'

Ophelia got her phone and typed in the GPS coordinates.

'You're driving us to Manchester. It should take ninety minutes.'

Katrina blew smoke into the air. 'Why Manchester?'

'I have a unit on an industrial estate on the outskirts. We'll dispose of the body there.'

'We?'

'Unless you want to stay here.'

Katrina laughed. 'Get in the car while I lock the house.'

Ophelia was checking her dark web account as Katrina slid into the driver's seat.

'The client paid in full.'

'The one who hired you to kill Duff?'

'Yes. I thought they wouldn't after what happened here.'

'Why?'

'Whoever paid me to kill Duff must have also put a contract out on me – that's how Darknight64 followed us here from Duff's house. So I assumed they wouldn't pay the rest of the Duff contract.'

'I've got a million and one questions.'

Ophelia switched the radio on. 'Let's get going. You can ask me all you want on the way.'

They headed out of the estate towards the M62 as Ophelia found Siouxsie and the Banshees' version of *The Passenger*.

'Does the client for the Duff contract have a name?'

Ophelia smiled. 'I still think it might be you.'

Katrina shook her head. 'And I told you I'm up to my eyeballs in debt. Plus, I was ready to kill the bastard myself.'

The anger and despair in her voice convinced Ophelia she was telling the truth. But there were still things she was unsure about with the grieving mother.

'You said your employer sacked you and your husband when they caught you stealing from them.'

'That's right.'

'So, are you under police investigation for that?'

Katrina's face darkened. 'They dropped it when Laura died.'

Silence engulfed them as the car hit the motorway.

'Are you okay with disposing of the body?'

Katrina shrugged. 'What choice do I have?' An instrumental electronic tune drifted out of the radio. 'How does the client know Duff is dead?'

'I sent them photos.'

'Does this mean you can trace them through the messages in Hitsville?'

'No. They run all communication through several anonymous Russian servers.'

'So we're stuck, then?'

'Maybe not. Most Hitsville members use a broker for their contracts, and that broker moderates a chatroom for those who pay a grand a month to access it.' She flicked at the screen, logging in to that service. 'It's a long shot, but worth a try.'

She sent a private message to the Hitsville broker.

Completed contract for Ripley79.

Shortly after, attacked by Darknight64.

Do you know who the client is?

Katrina glanced at Ophelia's phone. 'Ripley79 paid you to kill Duff?'

Ophelia put her phone away. 'Yes.'

'Ripley's a character from the 1979 movie, *Alien*.'

They sped past the sign to Huddersfield. 'That's before my time. And I only watch romantic comedies.'

'Are you a sociopath?'

Ophelia laughed. 'You think I'm a sociopath?'

'You murder strangers for money – isn't that the definition of a sociopath? I had good reason to kill Duff; you didn't.'

'Fifty grand is a good enough reason for me.' She glanced at the world passing them by. 'And anyway, sociopaths have no regard for right and wrong, while I do. And they can't function normally in society, which doesn't apply to me.'

'Do you have empathy?'

Ophelia grinned. 'Abso-fucking-lutely.'

'So you know that murder is wrong?'

'There's a lot to unwrap in that question, Katrina, and I don't know if now is the right time for a philosophical discussion about the rights and wrongs of killing somebody.' She pressed a finger into her reflection in the car window.

'But I'll tell you the only good advice my mother ever gave me: never let someone else's pain impede your pleasure.'

As Ophelia's phone pinged with a new message, Rufus Wainwright warbled across the airwaves. She removed it from her pocket and read it.

That's privileged information, Rossetti. You know that.

She replaced the phone.

'Good news?' Katrina said.

'I can't discover who put the hit on me.'

'What about tracing the payments to your bank?'

Ophelia considered it. 'Possibly.'

'What do you spend your ill-got gains on, if you don't mind me asking?'

'No, I don't mind,' Ophelia said. 'It might help me think about who's trying to kill me.' She turned the volume up on the radio as The Rolling Stones struggled to get what they wanted. 'I collect comic books.'

Katrina peered at her through amused eyes.

'Comics? Like *The Beano* and *The Dandy*?'

'No. American comics, Marvel mainly. Most of what I collect is expensive. Whenever I kill someone, I think about a rare issue of *The X-Men* or *The Avengers*.'

'I've seen the movies. What's the most you've spent on a comic?'

'A hundred grand.'

Katrina whistled loudly. 'Wow. Give it to me and I'll pay my debts.'

Ophelia scrutinised her. 'Are you still gambling?'

'There's a dead man in the boot and I'm driving down the motorway next to a killer. So what do you think?'

'I think I need a drink.'

Katrina reached into her bag and removed a pack of cigarettes.

'Do you mind if I smoke?'

'No, go ahead.'

She lit the cigarette and dragged on it. Katrina went to open a window, but Ophelia stopped her.

'It's okay. I've always liked the smell. It reminds me of my father.'

'Is he like you?' Katrina said. 'A paid killer?'

Ophelia sucked in the smoke, enjoying its potency invading her lungs.

'He killed himself when I was twelve, and his family paid for it ever after.'

'I'm sorry. That must have been terrible for you.'

Ophelia glanced at her reflection in the window. 'He slit his throat in front of me.'

They were twenty minutes from their destination, and the silence engulfed them until Katrina spoke.

'Do you want to know how I started gambling?'

'Would it help you to talk about it?'

Katrina touched her cheek as she drove. 'Perhaps.'

'So tell me.'

'When I was a kid, my father used to take me to the pub, which was where I first saw the machine flashing lights at me like a Disney castle. I was mesmerised. I was too young to have my own money, but I bugged my old man, and he'd give me cash to shut me up. So that's where it all started.'

Ophelia gazed at her, knowing it hadn't ended yet. Then, the ping from her phone interrupted her thoughts. She read the text from the broker.

Darknight64 hasn't worked a job through us for six months.

She peered at the message before switching back to the GPS directions.

'More good news?' Katrina said.

'Our friend in the boot didn't get the contract on me through Hitsville.'

'So, what does that mean?'

'Whoever wants me dead had another way of contacting him.' She pointed at the windscreen. 'Take the next right and head towards the industrial estate.'

Katrina did as instructed. 'We need to find out who the hitman was, then?'

'There's that *we* again,' Ophelia said. 'Are we partners now?'

Katrina laughed. 'Why not? I've got nothing else in my life. And who's to say that bloke wasn't there to kill us both?'

Ophelia ignored the question as they headed through the gates.

'Go straight on and turn left at the bottom for unit 12.'

'How long have you had this place?'

Ophelia peered into the darkness. 'Three years.'

'What do you use it for apart from getting rid of dead bodies?'

'It's my holiday home.'

Katrina parked near the unit, and Ophelia got out of the car. She punched a six-digit security code into the box on the wall. The door opened and Katrina drove inside. Ophelia followed her in and closed the entrance. She flicked on the lights as Katrina joined her.

'It's cosy,' Katrina said.

Shelves lined the wall, containing tools, knives, an electric saw, and a chainsaw. Ophelia removed a plastic overall and gloves from a box.

'Do you know the best way to dismember a body?'

Katrina puffed out her chest. 'What? No. Is that what we're going to do?'

Ophelia opened the car boot. 'How do you think we'll get rid of him?'

'Bury him somewhere?'

'Too risky. Some animal might dig him up. The first rule of the assassination trade is if you can't make the kill look like an accident, ensure the body is never found.' The corpse was only a few hours old, but Ophelia had to squeeze her nose because of the smell. 'Give me a hand getting him up.'

Katrina grimaced as they dragged the tarp containing Darknight64 from the car to the far side of the unit. They dumped him on the table, and Ophelia pulled the cover off. Then she removed her phone and took photos of his face.

'Is this you keeping trophies of your kills?'

Ophelia frowned at her. 'I'm not a monster. These should help me identify him later.'

Katrina scrutinised their surroundings. 'Do you have facial recognition software here?'

'No. And I need something more powerful than the commercial stuff any old Joe might use.'

'Where will you get that?'

'I'll pay a visit to my former employers in Manchester once we've dealt with our mystery dead man. You can wait here for me.'

Ophelia moved towards the electric saw, but Katrina grabbed her arm.

'Hey! You're not leaving me here with a dismembered body.'

'I can't take you with me to the Agency.'

Katrina let go of her. 'The Agency? Do you temp for an assassination bureau?'

Ophelia checked the battery in the saw as she replied.

'The Agency is an intelligence organisation of the British government.'

'Like MI5 and MI6?'

'Not quite. Those organisations must answer to the rule of law – the Agency doesn't. So their agents can kill with impunity, and often do. There is no accountability because they keep their actions from the public. Only a few in the government know of the Agency's existence.'

Katrina glanced at the corpse. 'And you work for them?'

'Only as a freelancer. But I know someone at the Manchester office, and they should be able to discover who our mystery assassin is. But you'll have to stay here or in the car. Taking you inside will cause too many problems.'

'I'll wait in the car. I'm not staying here with a corpse.'

'No problem. Do you want to help with the dismemberment, or are you cleaning up after I've finished?'

Before Katrina could answer, there was a scream from outside.

Katrina nearly jumped out of her skin. 'Shit! That was a woman screaming.'

And it came again.

Ophelia put the electric saw down and went to the window, pulling the blind aside: four blokes towered over a young girl on the ground.

'We have to do something,' Katrina said at Ophelia's side.

'We can't draw attention to ourselves.' Ophelia closed the blind. 'It's nothing to do with us.'

The girl screamed again, and the men laughed.

Katrina bared her teeth. 'We're not leaving her like that.' She grabbed a knife. 'I'll do it without you if I have to. I'm not afraid to die.'

Ophelia sighed. Then she put the saw on the body.

'You stay here. I'll deal with this.'

She went to the exit, opened it, and stepped outside. Four sets of feral eyes turned in her direction as the door closed behind her.

Perhaps I should have kept the saw.

4 KNOCK ON WOOD

The wind cut across Ophelia's face, loud enough to hurt her ears, but not prevent her from hearing their taunts.

'Have you come to join the party, skank?'

The bloke at the front carried a cattle prod, the blue light fizzing from the end as electricity burnt through the air.

'You've had your fun, boys, so why don't you go home now?'

'Stick her with the prod, Billy,' the skinny one said.

Billy stepped forward, pointing the weapon at her.

'Are you working with this other bitch? Have you got our merchandise in that unit?'

Ophelia watched the blue spark inching towards her. 'Merchandise?'

'Don't fucking mess around, you dumb bint.' He waved the prod at her. 'This is for cows like you and your mate on the ground.' He shook his head. 'Fancy these stupid mares thinking they could steal from us and get away with it.'

The others moved forward, leaving the girl behind

them. The scrawny one with yellow eyes and teeth to match spoke again.

'Now we've got two of them to play with, Billy. Can I go first for once?'

Billy turned and smacked him on the shoulder.

'Don't be fucking daft, Sam. You're the runt, and the runt of the pack always goes last.' The others laughed as they removed knives from their jackets.

Fuckety fucking fuck.

One stab of the prod and she knew she'd be helpless on the ground before them.

Ophelia glanced at the girl. 'It was too easy to steal from a moron like you, Billy. So, why don't you and your little mates fuck off before I shove that stick up your arse?'

He growled as he lunged at her. She dodged his clumsy attempt, and he bounced off the shutter behind her. The others didn't hesitate and jumped at her.

But they were slow, high on booze and drugs.

So she ran for the exit and the woods, rushing into the darkness, beyond the open ground. And away from Katrina.

Ophelia heard them behind her as she reached the trees, jumping over a branch as scrawny Sam hit it and fell into the dirt. She slipped into the shadows and turned, seeing the other three arrive, their faces illuminated by the blue fizzing from the cattle prod.

Billy grinned at her. 'Go on, lads. It's time for your fun.'

Two of them stepped over Sam, moving to flank her. Ophelia took a deep breath as the moonlight glinted in their eyes. She inched away, pushing through broken branches and thick grass. A gust of wind swept through them, snatching leaves from the trees and showering the men as if they were the happy couple at a wedding. Nature's gifts obscured their vision and gave Ophelia her chance. She jumped on the downed tree between them, using it to push off and kick the closest in the chest. He stumbled back as she landed in the dirt, swivelling her hips to bring her foot around and take the legs from under the other one. He joined his mate in the mud as she stood over them.

Can I scare them enough so they'll leave the girl and me alone?

Then Sam came roaring towards her, swearing as he lunged, arm outstretched, ready to slit her throat.

She sidestepped him, and he landed on the ground with the other two. Ophelia turned away, searching for Billy and his dangerous blue light, but she couldn't see him.

'You've killed Sam, you fucking bitch.'

Ophelia saw the skinny one with the knife sticking out of his gut, the blood turning the grass red.

Fuck. Now, what do I do?

The other two staggered to their feet, and she decided. She jumped behind the closest one, placed her arm around his throat and snapped his neck. Then she threw the body at the other thug as he charged at her. They crashed to the ground together. Ophelia snatched the knife from Sam's gut and thrust it into the other one's stomach. Then she wiped the handle clean and stood up.

It was just in time for the cattle prod to dig into her hip. Electricity jolted through her. The spasm started at the point of impact before shooting through every part of her. Ophelia's legs gave way as her head shook and drool dribbled from her mouth. She collapsed to the ground and joined the bodies there. Her blurred vision didn't stop her seeing Billy towering over her.

'How does a stupid snatch like you kill three of my men?' He spat into the trees. 'I'll admit that Little Sam was a waste of space, but the others were my best soldiers.' He kicked at her trembling foot. 'You and that other bitch have cost me a lot tonight. Still, I'll see what you've hidden in your unit. Then I'll put that other skank and you to work. How many blokes do you want fucking you every day? You're feisty, so I'll have to tie you to the bed, but I bet you could take thirty or more, eh?' He booted her again. 'You might even get to enjoy it, but I doubt it.'

Ophelia bit into her lip and tasted blood. She dug her fingers into the dirt, was pushing her aching bones up when he stabbed her with the prod. This time, he stuck it into her stomach, the volts frying her flesh, making her spasm in agony. She writhed on the ground, watching him leer as the leaves fell over her. More of her blood slipped down her throat as she struggled to speak.

'You know I'm going to kill you for this.'

His head was close to hers, the smell of cheap aftershave attacking her senses. The flickering electricity of the cattle prod was only inches from her eyes.

'Darling, you can barely move. And if you did, I'd only shock you again. So now, will you tell me how you and the other skank got a grand's worth of pills out of my stock? Did you stick it up your arses? Was that it?'

Ophelia sank into the damp mud beneath her, yearning for sleep.

'You did all this for a few drugs? You're even stupider than you look.'

He arched his back before sitting on her, his weight squashing against her guts. He moved the cattle prod around and laid its middle against her throat. His knees pushed her arms into the earth, her hands trembling as she struggled to breathe.

'I should kill you and leave you here.' He took a deep breath. 'But, I've got to take the other bitch back, so you might as well come.' He ran his fingers through her hair. 'I've always liked redheads.'

She snapped her head up to bite his hand, but he pulled it away from her.

'If I can find it, I'll snap your fucking pecker off.'

He grinned at her like a demented clown. 'That's my girl.' He got up and stood over her. She wished she had the strength to kick him in the balls. 'The lads will have a good time with you, like riding one of those electrical bulls on holiday. We might have to remove your teeth first, though, with you being a biter.' He pointed the prod at her. 'Better give you another jolt of this before I drag you back to the other bitch.'

She reached out a trembling hand to protest, but he shocked her in the shoulder, leaving it there longer than the other times. Her eyelids flickered, and then closed as he grabbed her arm.

But she didn't black out as Billy dragged her through the mud, hauling her to the unit. The young woman was still there, sobbing on the ground. He dumped Ophelia against the wall, her shoulder cracking as she hit the concrete. She shook her head and glared at him.

'I'd kill you slowly if I had the time, Billy Boy, but I guarantee it won't be painless.'

He pointed the cattle prod at her eye. 'Give me the code for the unit, or I'll burn your eyeball from the socket.'

She spat blood onto the ground. 'Do your worst, shit bag.'

He smirked at her. 'I believe you'll never tell me, no matter what I do to you. So I think you need more motivation.'

Billy grabbed the crying woman by the hair.

'No,' she screamed.

He dragged her to Ophelia. 'You can give me the code, or I'll torture her before you.'

She stared at the girl, and then gave him what he wanted. He punched in the numbers and the door opened. Then he grabbed Ophelia's arm and threw her inside. She hit the wall and slumped to the ground.

'Fucking hell,' she said.

He stood over her with the electricity sparkling from the prod.

'You'll be getting fucked all right, bitch. Hundreds of times and in every hole, once I find what you've got hidden here.'

Ophelia heard the chainsaw before she saw it. He was slower than her, turning as Katrina brought the blade down on his neck. The blood spurted out of him like a waterfall, landing on Ophelia's legs as his head popped off his shoulders and bounced over the ground, rolling up to Ophelia and resting near her arm.

'I think I'm getting the hang of this,' Katrina said.

Ophelia staggered up. 'The chainsaw or killing people?'

Katrina turned the power off and put the chainsaw down. Everywhere smelt of blood.

'Both. What happened to the others?'

Every part of Ophelia ached. 'Dead in the woods.' She went to the young woman sitting on the ground with her arms wrapped around her legs. 'Are you okay?'

She gazed at the two women. 'Is Billy dead?'

'Him and the others won't bother you again.' Ophelia helped her up. 'Can you make your way home?'

The woman nodded. 'Yes.' She smiled at Ophelia and walked out of the industrial estate.

'I thought you didn't leave any witnesses?' Katrina said.

'It doesn't matter now,' Ophelia said. 'She doesn't know who we are, and I won't be coming here again.'

'There's nothing in here that can lead back to you?'

'No. But you'll have to help me remove the bodies.'

Katrina shrugged. 'Okay. Where are they going?'

Ophelia nodded towards the trees. 'We'll put them in there with the others. When the police turn up, they might think the deaths were gang-related.'

'Including Darknight64?'

'Hopefully,' Ophelia said. 'Now, let's get Billy's head.'

5 FOOD FOR THOUGHT

Katrina peered out of the car window. 'My parents met around here.'

'In Manchester?'

'At the Hacienda nightclub. It's all apartments now.' She gazed into the early morning gloom. 'This Agency of yours has an office here?'

Ophelia nodded. 'They're not my Agency. I only freelance for them, but I know someone in this field office. It's in that building across the road.'

Katrina looked at it. 'I thought you said they were a super-secret organisation?'

'They're masquerading as an insurance company here.'

Katrina laughed. 'Maybe you should get some for me while you're there.'

Ophelia glanced at the bag at their feet.

'Remember to do as we agreed. Take what's in there for your debts and mortgage. Okay?'

'Do you always keep a hundred grand in storage units?'

'Just that one.' The money was the only thing she'd taken: that and the bodies.

'You've got blood on your trousers.'

Ophelia peered at the stain. 'It's Billy's.' She scrutinised her unexpected new partner. 'Are you okay?'

Katrina had killed two people in a matter of hours, the last by decapitation with a chainsaw. Not to mention the loss of her daughter and husband. Her emotional state must have been fragile.

'I'm fine. Are you sure I can't come with you?'

'It's best if you stay here. You don't want to be on the Agency's radar if you can help it. Especially after your recent exploits.'

'No problem. Is there anywhere here to eat? All that violence has made me ravenous.'

'There's an all-night McDonald's nearby.'

They stepped out of the car, and Ophelia pointed Katrina in the right direction. Then she crossed the road and walked to the entrance of the insurance company that was really the most secret of government intelligence organisations. Most people would have assumed the place would be empty, but she knew otherwise. So she rang the buzzer and got an immediate answer.

'Who is it?'

'Delivery for Cantona.'

She hoped the code hadn't changed since her last visit. The lock clicked and the door opened. She went up one flight of steps, stopping at the electronic security. She passed through that unscathed to be greeted by two armed guards.

'I need to see Agent Moore.'

The walls were bare, but she knew hidden cameras studied every part of her, electronic devices analysing the phones in her jacket. Her escorts didn't speak as they took her further into the building, one in front and one behind. It was a short walk through dark corridors before they ushered her into a room. It contained a table and two chairs, nothing else. And the concealed cameras. She sat and waited, reflecting on everything that had happened to her since crashing that party.

Whoever hired me to kill Duff employed somebody to wait for me there and murder me.

Then there was Katrina. A grieving mother and widow, now an accomplished killer. Ophelia pictured her sitting in McDonald's, stuffing fries into her mouth.

What's going through her mind right now? She probably needs counselling, not being taken on a murderous road trip.

We're not Thelma and Louise.

It's fine. Once I find out who Darknight64 was, she can return to Leeds with that money and pay off her debts. So she won't be my problem then.

Ophelia was thinking about that when the door opened and Alan Moore walked in. That wasn't his real name, just something he'd chosen when they'd first met because he realised she collected comics.

He smiled at her. 'Early start, Ophelia?'

She removed the phone from her jacket. 'I need you to find somebody for me.'

Moore sat at the table. 'We don't work for you. Or have you forgotten that?'

'A favour for a favour. You do this for me and I'll owe you. And you know how valuable my services are.'

He peered at the ceiling and she noticed the communication device in his ear. After thirty seconds of silence, he returned his focus to her.

'What do you require?'

She flicked at her phone and opened the images of Darknight64.

'I want to know who this is. Can you do that for me?'

He pulled the mobile towards him and went through the photos.

'Is he dead?'

Ophelia nodded. 'The police will find him sometime today, but I doubt they'll be able to identify him. Nevertheless, I need his details sooner rather than later.'

Moore considered her words, but she guessed he was listening to somebody else.

'Okay. I'll copy these photos and get back to you.'

He took her phone and left. Ophelia sat there and remembered the first time she'd worked for the Agency. They'd contacted her using Hitsville and set up a meeting in London. She took all her usual precautions, but knew something was different about it even before getting there. No two contracts were ever the same – she'd killed cheating husbands, gangsters, rapists and farmers – but this contract felt off to her. However, it was for half a million pounds up front, and she'd been prepared to take the risk.

So then, in a dive bar in Harrow, she learnt of the Agency and what they did to protect Britain and her citizens.

But even they couldn't get involved in the murder they were willing to pay her for.

An operative of a foreign power – that was their words – had organised the assassination of a Member of Parliament six months before. Ophelia remembered seeing it all over the news.

'I thought that was an individual acting on their own?' she'd said to the woman in that bar.

'No. It was just made to look like that.' The Agency knew who the mastermind of the murder was, but they had no proof, and it was too risky to send one of their agents abroad to kill this man.

So that's why they hired Ophelia.

She'd taken the job, but it had proved trickier than expected. She still had the scar on her back as a reminder of how it nearly all went wrong. As she thought about that, she checked her bruises from the cattle prod. Her hip and stomach were developing delicate shades of purple and blue.

Moore returned, carrying papers. 'More war wounds?'

'That was quick,' Ophelia said.

He placed the documents on the table and sat opposite her.

'No, it will be a while until we get a hit on your mystery bloke. This is your favour to us.'

She picked up a photo of a dark-haired, nervous-looking man.

'What is it?'

'That's Martin Cromwell. We need you to kill him.'

She put the photo down. 'Okay. What's the hitch?'

Moore separated the files, showing her a photo of luxury apartments.

'Cromwell has information harmful to the British government, which he's about to sell to the highest bidder. He's holed up at a gated community in Miami. We need you to get inside, recover any electronic or digital devices he has and make his death look like a suicide.'

'Why can't you have one of your American contacts handle this?'

He sighed. 'The information Cromwell has is something we don't want the Americans to see. We were about to send an Agency team there when you walked through our door. So you do this for us, and we'll tell you everything we discover about your mystery man.'

Ophelia considered the offer and thought about Katrina sitting at McDonald's.

It might be good to leave the country for a while with somebody trying to kill me.

She glanced at the photo of Cromwell again.

And it doesn't look like it will be an arduous job.

'How difficult is it to get into this gated community?'

'There's a full-length golf course in the middle, surrounded by two hundred individual homes. Each of them contains an up-to-date security system – meaning you need handprint and retina scans to get inside if you're not a resident. Cromwell doesn't play golf, so he only goes out to the closest supermarket in the facility. He does this twice a week, flanked by Russian flunkies as he has a slice of apple pie and flicks through the latest magazines. You only get into the community if you're a resident or invited by one – and the invitations go through a strict vetting process.'

'What about the essentials? Who delivers the mail and the food? Who fixes any faults? And I'm guessing the golf course staff don't live there.'

'Correct on the last one. They bus the workers in daily, and they've all had rigorous security checks. All deliveries go to the front gate and are brought in by guards, who only pass them on to authorised employees.'

Ophelia puffed out her cheeks. 'It sounds easier to break into Fort Knox. So how did the Russians get Cromwell inside?'

'Easy. They bought a property there, costing a cool million dollars. So if you've got the money to buy your way inside, the owners are happy to let you straight through.'

'Do we have the cash to do that?'

Moore shook his head. 'Nope.'

Ophelia smiled. 'You're going to parachute me in?'

He laughed. 'I hadn't thought about that, but it might be worth trying.'

'The residents who travel in and out – are their cars checked at the gate?'

'Only if they have non-residents with them,' Moore said. 'But they know if they're caught smuggling people in without authorisation, they void the warranty on their property. So the house reverts to the owners and they're kicked out – it's happened a few times to blokes trying to sneak hookers into the place.'

She nodded. 'Okay. Can you get me a list of all the residents and their timetables for coming and going?'

'Sure,' Moore said. 'I'll book your flights there and back and sort out a hotel near the airport where you can rent a car. How much time will you need?'

Ophelia considered how long it would take to select the right mark. Then the time she'd require for the job inside the facility, including dealing with any Russian security and getting out.

'Book the hotel for seven days under the usual name I use for Agency jobs.'

He scribbled notes onto a piece of paper. 'Is there anything else you need before I set this in motion?'

Ophelia pulled at her hair. 'Send somebody in to cut my locks – I'm due for a change.'

Moore smiled and stood. Then he left her to wait.

And she suddenly got the urge for a Big Mac.

6 SHE'S LOST CONTROL

While Ophelia was getting a trim and dye in the Agency basement, she sent Moore off for a few more essentials for her trip to the States. By the time he returned, she was admiring her new look in the mirror.

He handed her the documents. 'Do you want the information on your mystery man when I get it, or will you wait until you return to the UK?'

She admired the confidence he had in her. 'Best if we keep radio silence while I'm working.'

Moore agreed as he escorted her out of the building. 'Are you still collecting American comics?'

Ophelia put the folder under her arm as she stepped outside.

'One day, they'll pay for my retirement.'

He grinned at her as she left, and she guessed he thought the idea of her retiring was ridiculous.

You don't hear of many sixty-year-old assassins. Maybe they get killed well before that.

She strode past the car, heading towards the all-night McDonald's. It was empty when she got there apart from a bloke in the corner stuffing fries in his mouth. She couldn't see Katrina. Ophelia considered where she might have got to as she ordered a Big Mac meal with a large Coke. She sat near the window and peered into the Manchester gloom.

'Which butcher cut your hair?' Katrina said as she came out of the toilets and sat opposite her.

Ophelia pulled at her new haircut. 'You don't like it?'

Katrina grinned at her. 'I'm only joking. It looks great, very stylish, but why did you get it? It's not much of a disguise if you think the coppers are after us.'

Ophelia pushed the folder out of the way as a server brought her order over. She sucked Coke into her mouth through a paper straw, knowing the sugar would keep her awake. Her flight to Miami was in six hours. She'd sleep on the plane since it was a twelve-hour journey. She opened the folder and removed the passport.

'I'm going abroad for a few days. You should return to Leeds and sort your house out.'

'You mean clean up the blood?'

Tomato sauce dripped over Ophelia's lips as she bit into the burger.

'That would be a start.'

'Does this trip have anything to do with our mystery hitman?'

'It's a favour for a favour. I should know who Dark-night64 was by the time I return.'

Katrina stole one of her fries. 'And then?'

'Then I'll see why he tried to kill me.'

'What about me?'

Ophelia slurped on the Coke. 'What about you?'

'Is this the end of our partnership?'

Ophelia peered deep into her eyes, knowing this should be the last time she saw the other woman, but something strange gnawed at her heart: guilt for getting Katrina involved in her life and turning her into a double murderer.

'I'll contact you when I return. How does that sound?'

Katrina smiled. 'Fantastic. What will you bring me back from America?'

'How do you know where I'm going?'

Katrina pointed at the paper sticking out of the folder. 'That's got a Miami address.'

Ophelia pushed the papers aside and changed the subject.

'How are you feeling?'

'Do you mean about losing my daughter and husband?' Ophelia nodded. 'I'll never get over Laura's death. This may sound heartless, but I don't think much about Brian. We might have been living together, but we'd lived separate lives for a long time. I knew he was seeing somebody else, but I didn't care. It was sad what happened to him, but I'm not heartbroken. Do you know what I mean?'

'Feeling nothing for dead people is what I do, Katrina.'

'I guess, but you must care about somebody, surely? Even Hitler and Stalin had people they loved.'

Ophelia spat a fry onto the table. 'Are you comparing me to the biggest mass murderers in history?'

Katrina shook her head. 'No, but, well, you know what I mean. Everybody needs somebody to connect to. We go mad otherwise.'

'Who's to say I'm not already mad?'

'Are you sure you're not a sociopath?'

'Psychologists now refer to it as an antisocial personality disorder. I've taken no tests, but it's possible whatever I am was passed on to me through my mother.'

'Is she a paid assassin?'

Ophelia laughed. 'She's an exceptionally cold woman.

If there's a human form of the iceberg that sank the *Titanic*, it would be her. My mother believes she's descended from the Romanovs, the Russian royal family murdered by the Bolsheviks in 1918. The resentment has festered in her for years, making for a tough childhood, especially combined with my father's depression and mania.'

And alcoholism. Don't forget that.

Katrina crushed a fry between her fingers. 'My grandparents were Holocaust survivors, children surviving a horror their parents didn't. This was on my mother's side; even though she was born years after the war ended, I know it damaged her. But she was a loving mother.'

'And your father?'

Katrina sighed. 'He had the weight of the world on his shoulders, so he had little time for me. And he was a gambler.'

'Perhaps that's where you got it from.'

'Possibly. Brian was very much like my dad, so maybe that's why I ended up with him.' She peered at Ophelia. 'You're not close to your mother?'

Ophelia wiped tomato sauce from her lips. 'God knows where my mother is. The last I heard, she'd joined a cult.'

'A cult?'

'Yeah, it's probably the best place for her, but I think they're in for a shock.'

'How so?'

Ophelia finished the Coke. 'My experience with cults is limited, but they usually manipulate people to follow their twisted beliefs. My mother is a social predator who has charmed and manipulated her way through life, leaving behind a trail of broken hearts, shattered expectations and empty bank accounts. She'll be running that cult by now.'

A couple stumbled into the McDonald's, staggering to the counter. Ophelia watched them as Katrina spoke.

'Do you think you might have inherited some of your mother's unusual behaviour?'

'Are you back to thinking I'm a sociopath?'

Katrina shook her head. 'I'm only curious about how you got to this point.'

'What, eating junk food in the early morning with a killer?'

Katrina grinned. 'Yeah, I guess I'm one to talk about sociopaths.'

Ophelia crushed the Coke cup in her hand.

'It's different for you. You killed to protect me. You don't have an antisocial personality disorder. Sure, a gambling addiction, but that's not the same thing.'

'Maybe I should come with you to the States.'

'What, so I can drop you off in Las Vegas?'

Katrina frowned. 'That's uncalled for.'

Ophelia didn't apologise. 'No. You go home, and I'll call you when I get back.'

Before Katrina could reply, the couple sat next to them.

'Would you ladies like to earn some easy money?' the bloke said.

Fatigue seeped through Ophelia. The Coke hadn't done its job. She looked at the man; the haze in his eyes matched his trembling hands.

'Go away,' Ophelia said.

'How much cash?' Katrina said.

'A hundred quid each,' the woman said. She had a bird's nest haircut and smelt like two-day-old bacon.

Katrina rubbed at her nose. 'What do we do for that?'

The bloke glanced around the empty McDonald's. 'I'll tell you when we get there.'

His arm twitched, knocking the folder on the floor, scattering the photos and papers everywhere. Ophelia scowled, kneeling to collect the files. When she got up, the man was pointing a gun at Katrina's stomach.

'Are you desperate for drugs?' she said.

The bloke shook his head. 'Go outside, now.'

Ophelia sighed, doing as instructed. Katrina and she left together, with the man and woman behind them. If this messed up her flight to Miami, she'd be pissed off even more than she already was.

'Where to?' she said.

He pushed the gun into her spine.

'Keep walking to the bottom of the road and turn left into the alley.'

The street was empty. The gloom had turned into the early morning, and the taste of tomato sauce lingered in the back of her throat. She removed a piece of onion from her teeth. He pushed her against the wall. She heard somebody singing *Love Will Tear Us Apart* somewhere in the distance.

'Are we still getting the hundred quid?' Katrina said.

The man laughed. 'Maybe, if you do as you're told.'

Ophelia scrutinised them, recognising the mania in his face and the despair possessing the woman with him.

'Who are you?' she said.

He waved the gun at her. 'You can call us Laurel and Hardy.'

'Fine,' Ophelia said. 'That makes me Groucho, and my friend is Harpo.' She glanced at Katrina. 'So what do you two jokers want?'

'You need to get us into that building I saw you leaving,' he said.

She felt the cold wall behind her. 'Did you follow me from there?'

The woman spoke. 'We've been there since last night. You have to get us inside.'

'Why?' Katrina said.

The bloke aimed the weapon at her. 'They took our son. He's only fifteen, and they grabbed him from us in the night.'

'What's he done?' Ophelia said.

The man scowled at her. 'Nothing. They say he's a terrorist, but that's nonsense. He's a teenager, for God's sake.'

The wind cut across Ophelia's face. 'He must have done something.'

The woman wiped a tear from her cheek. 'He goes nowhere, always in his room on the computer. He's got school and us, that's it.'

Ophelia took a deep breath. 'It's not my problem. Leave before I take that gun from you and break your arm.'

Katrina stepped from the wall. 'We'll help you, but you'll have to wait a few days. The Agency won't let Groucho back into the building until she completes a job for them.'

Ophelia scowled at Katrina.

'The Agency?' the woman said.

Katrina smiled at her. 'It doesn't matter. We'll help you, but you must give us some time.'

The man wasn't convinced, waving the gun around.

'No, I don't believe you. We have to get inside that building now.'

Ophelia had had enough. She stepped forward and took the pistol from him before he could move. He tried to protest, but she pushed him into a pile of rubbish. She left him there and headed out of the alley.

Katrina rushed to her. 'Won't you help them?'

'We haven't got time for this,' Ophelia said. She slipped the gun into her pocket. 'You go home and I'll get a taxi to the airport.'

Katrina shook her head. 'If you don't help them, I will. Losing a child is the worst thing in the world.'

Ophelia looked between her and the woman helping the man up.

'What will you do for them?'

'I don't know. I'll make it up as I go along. It's worked for me so far.'

Ophelia took a deep breath and walked away. Then she turned to look at Katrina.

'Don't do anything until I get back.'

7 BREATHING

Ophelia's earliest memory was of her mother driving the family car into a tree. Her father was in the passenger seat and she was in the back, trying to remove her seatbelt when she looked up to see her mother smiling.

Then she saw the branches reaching out for her.

The screech of the tyres and Johnny Rotten's voice blaring out of the radio drowned out her father's scream. The window on her side was down, letting the wind blow in the smell of strawberries from a nearby field. Ever since that day, the strawberry aroma would remind her of the crash and the Sex Pistols singing about a holiday in the sun.

The seatbelt had stopped the impact from throwing Ophelia into the front seat, but it had cut into her stomach and drawn blood underneath her clothes. She still had the scar, joined by the others she'd gained over the years. The car was a mess, but the safety measures had saved all three of them from serious injury. She had a bruised knee while her father fractured his wrist. Her mother was unharmed. Ophelia sat in the field as her parents argued about the accident. But she knew it was no misfortune. Her mother had driven into the tree deliberately.

Did she want to kill us all? Or only hurt my father?

She remembered watching her parents as they waited for the police and the ambulance to arrive, studying their faces as if they were aliens just arrived on Earth. It was the first time she realised something was wrong between them. Ophelia was an only child, though she spent time with various cousins growing up. Observing her parents before her father's suicide, Ophelia got the distinct impression they must have ended up together by accident since they were complete opposites. She was cold and distant, whereas he was the life and soul of the party. Only later did Ophelia recognise his public effervescence as his way of hiding his genuine emotions.

Her parents had one thing in common: the utter self-belief they were better than others. They had married young, both of them twenty-two, having Ophelia three years into the marriage. They had met at university, him going into politics while she became a lawyer. They didn't lack money. Her mother worked in a small-time law firm before starting her own practice two years before her husband's death. Sometimes she'd take her daughter into the office with her, where Ophelia would watch as her mother became rich by helping the guilty avoid punishment.

'One day, you'll be like me,' her mother would say.

Those days in her mother's office were some of the few times they spent together. However, her mother never treated her like a daughter, and Ophelia wondered why she was even there. That was until she realised it was because her mother wanted Ophelia to see how she behaved towards her staff. They were less than nothing to her, cogs in a machine to be replaced if they didn't satisfy her needs.

'It's important to know your place in life, Ophelia.'

Her father presented himself as a good man in his political work, spending hours and days striving to improve the lives of others. Yet, he'd spend little to no time with his only child. And Ophelia knew he was unfaithful to his wife. She'd heard his whispered phone calls and saw him kissing another woman not long before his suicide. She'd always wondered if his infidelity had contributed to his decision to kill himself in front of her.

The only benefit she got from her father was raiding his music collection. As a result, she learned more from Iggy Pop, Lou Reed, and Janis Joplin than from her parents.

Ophelia never wondered if her genetics or upbringing influenced her line of work. Even with her emotionally unstable parents, she still had a comfortable life, never wanting for anything apart from encouragement and love. She was successful at school, and there was talk she might follow her mother's example and pursue a law degree. Ophelia knew that would never happen.

At home, inside a six-bedroomed mansion in the countryside, there were others to look after her, including several nannies. Pets were forbidden to her, and the meetings with her cousins were rare. It meant the only time she spent with other kids was at school, and even most of them gave her a wide berth. Her intellectual superiority and unusual behaviour kept most pupils at a distance from her.

Becoming a paid assassin was an accident. She'd got into a few fights with kids as a teenager, but never hurt a fly until she broke a mugger's neck one night. He approached her as she walked through a park, grabbing her waist and throwing her to the ground. The bloke wasn't much bigger than her, so she found it easy to place her arm around his neck and throw him over when he tried to get on top of her.

And that's when he landed awkwardly. The snap of the bone was loud enough to scare the birds from the trees, and the sound still lingered in her thoughts.

If she'd called the police, Ophelia assumed she could have claimed it was self-defence and an accident, but she didn't hang around. Instead, her satisfaction from it filled her mind with thoughts of murder and death just as a mystery illness struck her down. The euphoria from killing the mugger soon evaporated, her brain awash with clogged synapses, which affected the rest of her until she woke up one day and couldn't hear anything. It was during her last few weeks of school, only taken up with exams. The clock was flashing and the radio should have been inside her ears, but nothing was there.

Ophelia stumbled out of bed, thinking it was a dream, staggered to the bedroom door, and opened it. Her mother was at work, so she shouted for a servant, shocked when she couldn't hear her own voice. She was clutching at her throat when she stood on something. After that, all she remembered was crashing down the stairs until she hit the bottom.

She was lying on the sofa when she woke, peering at her mother's distressed face.

'I was called from an important meeting for this,' her mother said. 'Are you high?' Ophelia couldn't speak, but shook her head. 'Well, Stella will take care of you.'

Then her mother turned and left. Stella was the cook, and she didn't look too happy to be caring for a sick teenager. Eight hours later, Ophelia was in the Intensive Care Unit in the hospital.

Even now, she remembered little from that time. Most of it was spent hearing her mother's bitter voice or in hallucinatory dream states. Sometimes she'd be playing an actor in one of her favourite movies – Emma Watson as

Hermione in the *Harry Potter* series – or a character in a science fiction novel or comic book. She became a Valkyrie escaped from Valhalla, fighting hordes of trolls and demons. The demon leader had the face of her mother, while the thing whimpering at her bloodstained feet was Ophelia's father.

She also dreamt of school and being the most popular girl there. But then that fantasy would unravel and she was alone in the schoolyard as a thousand kids beat her to a pulp. Then the scene would transform into her floating above the ground, watching as her father slit his throat for the millionth time. As soon as the blood covered everything, she'd drop into a crimson river as his dead eyes burned into her soul and he spoke to her.

'Who's disease will you inherit, Ophelia? Mine or your mother's?'

She tried to speak, but nothing came out apart from a strangled gasp. Eventually, he would melt into the liquid at her feet, disappearing into a sea of red.

Then there was the recurring vision of the mugger attacking her. Only this time, it was he who killed her. She'd lie in that hospital bed, feeling the man ripping her body apart, the pain shooting through every inch of her. His fingers were around her neck, choking Ophelia as she jerked upwards, legs and arms flailing like a demented marionette. Several times, the nurses had to sedate her because of that nightmare.

When the visions disappeared, she saw the medical equipment hanging from her like umbilical cords; cold metal and plastic caressed her flesh more than her parents ever did. She spent six weeks recovering; no more visits from her mother until the doctors diagnosed her ailment.

'Poison,' a consultant said.

Ophelia's mother was wearing an expensive white suit, looking like a fallen angel.

'What type of poison?' she said.

The doctor's voice drifted inside Ophelia's head, resembling a radio broadcast from a distant star.

'It appears to be from the Amanita phalloides mushroom, commonly known as the death cap.'

Ice dripped from her mother's lips. 'Mushrooms?'

Ophelia lost consciousness before she could hear any more. She later learnt that the doctors believed the poison had come from mushrooms cooked in the kitchen. After that, she never saw Stella again, but she knew she'd been lucky to survive. Her liver was the primary target of toxicity from the death cap mushroom, but other organs, especially the kidneys, were affected. That's when Ophelia knew Lady Luck was looking down on her.

It took a long time to recover her physical and mental strength. But that experience and what had happened with the mugger set her on an alternative path in life. Ophelia promised herself she'd never be a victim again. Instead, she'd take her mother's cold indifference and use that to carve out a career in murder.

The other thing she took from her mother was money. A successful law firm meant she had the opportunity to sift through her mother's financial accounts, filtering a bit here and there using her considerable computer skills. Once she had enough, she never looked back at the family home or her remaining parent.

All she knew of her mother now came from the rumours online; that's how she'd heard about her joining the cult. She didn't know how she'd got involved with them or if her mother still had her law firm, but it was the cult members Ophelia felt sorry for.

But she'd left all that behind, dipping her toe into the shadowy world of dark web criminal activity and choosing isolation.

But now, she'd gained a sidekick.

Katrina. What should I do about her?

She knew what her mother would say. 'It's a weakness to rely on others.'

She'd heard those words so many times. And for once, she realised her mother was right.

So what to do about Katrina?

That thought occupied her mind all the way to the airport.

8 MIAMI

Ophelia peered at the ten-foot barrier surrounding Sunnyside Homes. She'd driven around it twice, discovering two gates, one at either end. From the details she'd got from Moore, she knew the resident she needed to get her beyond the wall had left at the weekend for his monthly trip to Las Vegas and would return tomorrow.

From a distance, she watched as guards stopped and questioned every driver entering and leaving, passing electronic sensors over each vehicle. She'd known that was part of the security process from Moore's information, understanding she wouldn't get inside by hiding in the boot of a car or truck. That was when Ophelia knew she'd need another way in and out, which was where the gambler came in.

Another gambler. How appropriate.

She observed the security for an hour before returning to the hotel, ordering room service and watching a true-crime documentary. It put her in the perfect mood for murder.

IN THE MORNING, she had breakfast in her room and checked the times for the flight arrivals from Las Vegas. The one she was interested in was on schedule, giving her plenty of time to be at the spot she'd selected on the road a mile outside Sunnyside.

As she finished her fried eggs, she looked again at the photo of the bloke she was about to hijack and blackmail into helping her: Joe Swanson. In his mid-fifties, Swanson was a tall, thin man who had been a successful investment banker before retiring to Sunnyside. He was single with no pets and only one hobby: gambling. Ophelia wondered if he was the type to gamble with his life.

Thirty minutes later, she was listening to ACDC on the radio while waiting for Swanson's car. She knew the make and the registration, but still hadn't figured out how she'd get him to stop.

I could stand in the middle of the road. That's worked before. Show a bit of leg. It confuses most blokes.

Yet, at other times, it had also nearly got her killed. So, it was too risky. And he might just drive around her. The only way she could think would work would be if she parked her car as if it was a police roadblock. Then, she'd apologise and leave if any other vehicles turned up.

So that's what she did, only having to move once for a truck delivering groceries to Sunnyside before Swanson arrived ten minutes later. She smiled at him as he wound down the window, knowing from the sparkle in his eyes that he must have had an excellent weekend in Vegas.

'Have you broken down?' he said.

She removed the knife she'd taken from the hotel and stuck it close to his eye.

'Get out of the car, Joe.'

'What?'

'Don't make me repeat myself. I want you alive, but you don't need to have two good peepers for what I require.'

He did as instructed, stumbling out the door as fear gripped his face.

'You can have all the money I got, lady.'

She pushed him towards her car. 'Get in and shut up.'

Sweat trickled down his forehead as he got into the passenger seat. Ophelia joined him and drove off the road, parking behind some trees. She got out and told him to do the same. She ensured no other traffic was coming as she marched him back to his car. Then she removed a piece of paper from her pocket and showed it to him.

'What's this?' he said.

'Take it and read it.'

His fingers trembled as he read the information. 'This is a marriage certificate with my name on it.'

She nodded. Moore had supplied her with the document, and Ophelia had only needed to add the details once she knew who the mark was.

'It was a whirlwind romance, Joe – love at first sight. Made even more romantic since it happened in Vegas. Don't you think we make a good-looking couple? Especially me.'

He peered at the paper, then at her. 'You're Rosie Wilde?'

'Rosie Swanson now. And I'm looking forward to you taking me to my new home.'

'Why are you doing this? Is it a practical joke? Did David put you up to this?'

She shook her head. 'Your brother? No, this is nothing to do with him. Not yet, anyway.'

'What does that mean?'

She slipped the knife into her jacket. 'David, his wife and their kids will be fine if you do everything I tell you. Do you understand?'

His voice shivered. 'Who are you?'

Ophelia put her arm around his shoulder.

'I'm Rosie Swanson, your blushing new bride. You have to show them that certificate at the gate, and Sunnyside Homes should add me to their database.' She squeezed his arm. 'Don't worry, though. You can tell them it didn't work out in two or three weeks and wasn't legal, anyway. Then you'll continue your monthly trips to Vegas and those nights with that redheaded hooker you're obsessed with.'

It never ceased to amaze her the information the Agency could acquire. Joe appeared to accept it as a *fait accompli* as she led him to his car.

'What happens when we get inside?' he said as he started the engine.

She patted his leg. 'Don't you worry your pretty little head about that, husband. I shouldn't be staying at yours for too long, perhaps only a day. I'll have to tie you up and gag you, but I understand you're used to that. Think of it as a Vegas adventure in your home with the gamble being with your life.'

'Okay,' he whispered.

Ophelia turned the radio on and listened to Fleetwood Mac as he drove to Sunnyside. She whistled as they went through the countryside and approached the gate in the middle of the giant wall.

'Just act normal,' she said. 'Tell them about the marriage and how desperate you are to get me home.' She winked at him. 'Let them think it's time for our extended honeymoon.'

He nodded as he stopped at the security station. He wound down the window as the guard strode up to the car.

'Did you book ahead for a visitor, Mr Swanson?'

Swanson pulled at his collar. 'Well, Stan, it was completely unexpected.' He glanced at Ophelia, who was grinning at him. 'I got married in Las Vegas.'

'Married?' Stan said.

Swanson reached into his jacket and removed the marriage certificate.

'Yeah, this lady just swept me off my feet – it was a whirlwind romance.'

The guard took the paper, glancing through the document before staring at Ophelia.

'Ms Rosie Wilde?'

She produced her best hyena laugh. 'Wilde by name and by nature.' She winked at Stan. 'But I'm Rosie Swanson now.' She squeezed her fake husband's knee. 'And we haven't had a chance for a proper honeymoon yet, if you know what I mean.'

Stan's face turned a fine shade of pink.

'Right, I have to take a photo of this certificate and enter the details into the security database.' He puffed out his cheeks. 'And I'll need a picture of you, Mrs Swanson.'

Ophelia frowned as she stepped out of the car and went to him, putting her hand on Stan's arm and giving it a little squeeze.

'Oh, Stan, can we do that later?' She ran her fingers through her hair while hanging on to him. 'I just got a fresh cut and it's a proper mess. Once I sort it out, I'll get Joe to bring me right back here. I promise.'

Stan's head resembled a red apple and she felt him tremble.

'Err, I shouldn't really, but okay, for you.'

She let go of his arm and kissed him on the cheek. He blushed even more as he took the certificate into the security office, and she went to the car. She grinned at Swanson.

'I knew I'd enjoy living here.'

He didn't reply, a nervous laugh slipping from his mouth as Stan returned the paper. The flush had left Stan's face, but his voice was still trembling.

'Enjoy your honeymoon,' he said as they drove away.

Ophelia stared at the security cameras as they left, hoping they didn't record twenty-four hours a day. They went past luxurious houses, with the golf course on one side and shops on the other.

'What now?' Swanson said as he stopped outside his house and waited for the electronic garage to open.

She glanced out the window, seeing empty streets and gauging how far she was from Cromwell's property. She'd memorised the map, knowing which direction she needed to take between Swanson's place and Cromwell's.

They were safely inside when she replied.

'Are you hungry? I need a snack before I go to work.'

'What work?'

They got out of the car together. 'It's better if you don't know, Joe. Then you can deny everything later. Now show me where the kitchen is.'

He led her out of the garage and into the house, passing the living room and into the kitchen.

Swanson slumped against a chair. 'I need to go shopping, but a few things are in the fridge.'

Ophelia looked inside and found the contents wanting.

'Okay, I'll take a trip to the shops later. Show me the rest of the place.'

A large window in the living room looked out upon the golf course. Various stuffed animal heads were hanging on the walls, ranging from foxes to bears. Their glazed eyes peered at her and seemed to follow Ophelia around the room as she checked the place for potential problems. He must have noticed her staring at the deadheads.

'I used to go hunting before I moved here.'

'Well,' she said. 'There's something we have in common.'

'Do you want to talk about it?'

His words surprised her. She'd been a paid assassin for most of her adult life, and apart from her recent adventures with Katrina, she'd never spoken to anybody about it. The job meant she had no real friends to confide in, and even with casual relationships, romantic or not, it was difficult to talk about the things other people found interesting. What was the point of talking to somebody about the latest action movie or some crime show on Netflix when she'd spent the day strangling someone?

She stared at Swanson. 'No. Let's take a walk.'

It was time for her to go to work.

9 CLUB COUNTRY

Ophelia's plan was open to fluctuation. She'd initially thought to keep a low profile once entering Sunnyside, but after convincing Swanson to help her, she'd realised she wouldn't be killing Cromwell inside the gated community. Instead, she'd take him outside the walls and deal with him in some remote spot, after dealing with his Russian security. So it didn't matter who saw her as long as she wasn't with Cromwell.

The route to Cromwell's house took them past the golf course clubhouse, so she got Swanson to take them inside.

'I fancy a drink,' she said when he'd asked why. The real reason was her intention to find out what was going on with Cromwell's foreign security without mentioning his name to any Sunnyside residents.

She sipped a gin and tonic in the bar and gripped Swanson's hand. His discomfort amused her into squeezing his fingers as a couple in their fifties approached them. The man was balder than an egg, with teeth brighter than the sun.

'Joe, you old dog. Why didn't you tell us you were off to Vegas to get wed?'

He and the woman – Ophelia assumed she was his wife – sat beside them without being invited. Swanson cradled a glass of Coke in his hands.

'It wasn't planned, Fred.' He glanced at Ophelia. 'It was a whirlwind romance.'

The woman thrust her hand at Ophelia. 'Honey, you must be special if you can tame this horndog.'

Ophelia took her hand, feeling the wrinkles against her skin. 'Word travels fast around here.'

'Judy and I keep our ears close to the ground,' Fred said. 'You've got to ensure no undesirables get through the Sunnyside walls.'

'Undesirables?' Ophelia said.

Fred nodded. 'There's a reason the houses here are so expensive: so only the right people can live in Sunnyside.' He held out his hands and looked across the room. 'It's like being inside a separate country in the heart of America, where all the bad things are kept from decent, ordinary, hard-working folks.'

Ophelia put on her best innocent face. 'Gee, I hope I fit in okay since, you know, I'm not from around here.'

Judy squeezed up to her. 'Honey, you'll do just fine.' Ophelia smelt the bourbon seeping out of her skin. 'Is that accent British? I don't think I've heard that one before and I've watched every episode of *The Crown* three times.'

Ophelia placed a hand on her chest and grinned.

'Oh, I'm as far removed from royalty as possible. My upbringing was in a tiny seaside village in the northeast of England. The only king I ever met was the bloke who sold my father his car.'

Judy and Fred laughed while Joe Swanson shifted in his

chair. From the look in his eyes, Ophelia knew he was thinking this would be the best time for him to get away from her.

So she reached over and squeezed his thigh.

'Oh, this is wonderful,' Judy said. 'We can watch all the British TV shows together.'

Ophelia smiled. 'That would be delightful.' She glanced at Fred. 'I thought your mention of undesirables meant you didn't like strangers coming to Sunnyside.'

Fred finished his drink. 'Some foreigners are okay.'

'Are there many here?' Ophelia said.

Judy rubbed at the second of her chins. 'No, I believe you must be the first.'

Fred shook his head. 'You're forgetting, Judy, about those Russians we saw with that little guy in the store.' He turned to Ophelia. 'Actually, I think he might be British as well.'

'Russians?' Joe said.

'Two big fellas,' Fred said. 'They've been here a month. They or the little guy bought the end house on Brunel Street. I asked about them at the security gate, but the guards say it's all legitimate – they paid for the property in cash. I've seen them in the store. They don't speak much, but the big guys have Russian accents while the other fella,' he glanced at Ophelia, 'he doesn't sound like your lovely bride, but it's not an American accent, that's for sure.'

The conversation drew others to them. Ophelia ended up amongst several men and women in their fifties and sixties enjoying their retirement while putting the world to rights – or at least putting America to rights. They had more drinks as she ate steak and fries, and the talk turned to how good or bad their golf rounds had been. She stayed on the periphery of the chatter, only talking when somebody asked her or Joe about the wedding and what it was like in Vegas.

'How did you two meet?' Judy said while Fred stared at Ophelia as if she was one of those women who stick pornographic leaflets into the hands of tourists on the strip. She was about to answer when Joe cleared his throat.

'Rosie was a judge at the moustache contest.' He pulled at the thick hair over his lip. Ophelia laughed and played along.

'Doesn't Joe look like Magnum PI?' She grinned at the locals hanging on her every word. 'Not the recent remake, but the classic Tom Selleck look.'

'You don't seem old enough to remember the 70s, young lady,' Fred said.

Ophelia swigged on her drink. 'Everything's on repeat nowadays.'

Everyone laughed together before she listened to the older people reminiscing about their lost youth. She peered at the bags under their eyes and wrinkled flesh, wondering if she'd ever reach that stage in her life.

Perhaps there's a retirement home somewhere for former assassins, where dedicated killers swap war stories while sipping cocktails and complaining about their arthritis.

That thought amused her as she observed her fake husband, surprised at how he'd settled into the part of the abduction victim. It took her a while to realise he was enjoying the spotlight his new "bride" had brought him in this community.

It wasn't late when they left, but it was dark outside. Ophelia wrapped her arm in his and pulled Joe towards her.

'Why don't you give me a tour of the neighbourhood?'

The drink and the attention must have reignited his courage.

'Is this about the Russians? Is that why you're here?'

The warmth of his body contrasted with the chill of the evening wind. Still, strolling through Miami at night wasn't the same as the nights she'd spent in that northern village of her childhood. She peered at her surroundings, wondering how she'd got here from the starting point of seeing her old man slit his throat in front of her. That image was always with her, but she could push it far into the shadows of her mind most of the time. Yet now, it had rushed back to haunt her for unknown reasons.

Ophelia could see her father gazing deep into her eyes, watching him raise the knife and waiting for him to strike at her. Even years later, as she strolled through the Miami night, she still expected him to murder her with that blade. That's what she'd waited for then, recognising his mania when he'd staggered home, spotting the frustration in his face when he realised his wife wasn't there.

He was going to kill us all. I know it. But my mother's absence must have changed something in him. And that's why he took his own life and spared me.

But she still had no rational explanation or understanding of why he'd done it. Her mother always refused to talk about it, no matter how often Ophelia asked. That's why she'd settled on the theory it was to do with that woman she'd seen her father kissing. It had been a pure accident on Ophelia's part, stumbling into a darkened room of a club she was too young to attend, seeing the young woman in her father's arms. Several years after his death, she'd tried to track down the mystery woman, but had discovered nothing useful.

'Are you in the FBI or the CIA?'

Swanson's question brought her back into the present.

'What did I tell you about not knowing, Joe?'

He stopped walking, staring straight at her. 'You're not a terrorist, are you?'

She shook her head and laughed. 'Hey, Joe, where are you going with that terrorist in your hand?'

He pulled away from her. 'What?'

Ophelia peered over his shoulders, recognising they were outside Cromwell's house. The lights were on downstairs and in the front bedroom.

How do I get inside and deal with the Russians?

I could shove Joe up to knock on the door and invite ourselves in.

No – I need them out of the house.

She grabbed Swanson's hand. 'No, Joe, I'm not a terrorist. I promise I won't harm any American citizens while I'm with you.'

'So it is about the Russians?'

Seeing the confusion in his eyes made her think she should have tied him up in the house. So she lied to him.

'Yes, Joe. Those Russians are a threat to both American and British security. The people in the club were talking about that little guy with them. Do you remember?' He nodded. 'Well, that little guy is important to the Americans and the British. The Russians abducted him and brought him here. And it's my job to get him out.'

He inspected her face, and she guessed he was desperate to believe her. But he couldn't contain his doubts.

'Why don't the police or the security forces come and deal with them?'

'Look around you, Joe – this place is full of older people. It would be a slaughterhouse if the regular authorities stormed in here. Don't you see that?'

He thought about it for ten seconds before nodding.

'I suppose you're right, but why did they bring him here?'

She shrugged. 'I'm not sure. If I had to guess, I'd say it's to do with Sunnyside's high level of security. My information is that they're holding him here before they can ship him out of the country. And before you ask, I don't know why he's important.'

Ophelia observed him processing the details, recognising that his mind was trying to justify his lack of protest at what had happened since she'd hijacked him. If he convinced himself that all of this was for the good of the country and she wasn't a homicidal lunatic, then he'd feel better about himself.

Keep telling yourself everything will be okay, and it will be.

She knew how he was feeling. Several times in her early killing days, she'd rationalised her behaviour by thinking it was all to do with her dysfunctional parents and upbringing. Once she'd realised that murder was a guiltless exercise for her, she pushed all thoughts of trying to understand why she was like that deep below the memory of her father's suicide. But those thoughts had resurfaced with her conversations with Katrina and the notion she might be a sociopath.

Too many strange ideas are resurfacing at the wrong time.

Swanson was talking, but she wasn't listening; the voices in her head were from her father and Katrina.

What will I do about Katrina?

How does an ordinary woman turn into a multiple murderer overnight? It can't be purely down to what happened to her daughter.

And Katrina had shown no emotion after killing two people.

Perhaps she's a sociopath.

Somebody switched the lights off in the Cromwell house.

I must stop my mind wandering like this – I'm getting distracted. First, I'll get this job done, and then focus on who hired Darknight64 to kill me.

'How will you get the guy from the Russians?' Swanson said.

Ophelia saw the curtains twitch and considered the question. She squeezed his fingers and dragged him away.

'I'll know in the morning.'

'What happens now?'

She grinned at him. 'Why, Joe, it's time to enjoy our honeymoon.'

10 SPACE ODDITY

Ophelia woke early, showering before checking Swanson was okay since she'd gagged and tied him up as soon as they'd got back to the house. She dried her hair as she removed his gag.

'I need the bathroom,' he said.

Water dripped from her head. 'I need a dog.'

He grimaced as she undid his restraints. 'What?'

'Get cleaned up and changed while I make the breakfast. Then we're off to acquire a mutt – the smaller, the better. Are there any pet shops here?'

Swanson rubbed at his eyes. 'No, but I might know where we can borrow a dog for a bit. You're not going to kill it, are you?'

Ophelia laughed at him. 'I'm not a psychopath, Joe. Now, how do you like your eggs?'

TWENTY MINUTES LATER, they were eating scrambled eggs on toast. He was drinking coffee while she sipped water. She'd wanted a cup of strong tea, but he didn't keep any.

If I stay here more than today, I'll need to visit that community store.

She couldn't see how she'd get the job done in one day, so she needed the dog to help her. Swanson must have been reading her mind.

'How long are you going to be here?'

Ophelia licked the egg from the top of her lip. 'Two more days at the most, I hope. Why? Aren't you enjoying my company? You seemed to have a good time in the clubhouse last night.'

He slurped coffee. 'It's uncomfortable, being tied up like that. And it's hard to breathe with a gag in your mouth. I told you I'd be no trouble.'

She finished her breakfast. 'I wish I could trust you, Joe, but I can't. At least this way, you know I won't kill you by mistake.'

He gulped. 'What do you want a dog for?'

'You'll find out. Now show me where this beast is.'

He took her to one of his neighbours three doors down: Catherine Cole, a widow in her seventies. Catherine's daughter had bought her a poodle for company, but the old woman struggled to take it for regular walks, which is where Joe and Ophelia came in.

Once they got the dog, they walked it through the streets before ending up outside Cromwell's house. The mutt had pissed and shit its way around the estate, and it had amused her to see her fake husband cleaning up after little Daisy. Now, the pup was peering at her through large watery eyes.

Ophelia had wanted to have a pet, any animal, to have something to talk to that wasn't her parents when she was younger. Her mother had been indifferent to her daughter's needs, while her father gave her a hamster. She'd only had it a few days when it disappeared, and Ophelia guessed he'd disposed of it since he was always complaining about the noise it made running in its wheel.

Since then, she'd never kept pets, so it was unusual to see how Daisy had already grown attached to her. The little mutt was bouncing on its legs as if it was the most exciting day in its brief life. Its agitated state gave Ophelia an idea of how to use the dog to learn more about the situation in the Cromwell property. She dragged Daisy and Swanson across the road to the house, nudging the gate open to let the dog run into the garden.

'I'll get her,' Joe said.

Ophelia stopped him, watching Daisy run to the back. 'Can I trust you, Joe?'

His lips trembled as he smiled at her. 'Of course. I promise.'

She didn't trust him, but she had no choice.

'If you're not here when I return, you know what will happen.'

She left before he could reply, running after the dog. She glanced through the front window, seeing nobody inside. When she reached the back, Daisy was shitting on a gnome's head. Ophelia grimaced at the smell, moving beyond the mutt and reaching the door. She tried the handle, but it was locked. She peered through the window, seeing another empty room.

Then she heard voices in the street.

Ophelia ignored the stink and grabbed the dog. She inched her way to the front of the house, watching three men striding past Swanson – two massive blokes as wide as they were tall and a much smaller man with a nervous twitch.

The Russians and Cromwell.

They never looked back as she joined Joe, dropping Daisy to the ground.

'Did they speak to you?'

He shook his head. 'No, but both goons glared at me.'

She put the lead on Daisy. 'Okay. We'll follow them at a distance, so don't attract attention by doing anything stupid.'

Ophelia led the dog and her fake husband through Sunnyside, observing the targets.

Perhaps I'm missing a chance here by not returning to the house, getting inside and waiting for them.

That thought possessed her brain as she dragged Daisy and Swanson strode next to her in silence. She observed the Russians, watching as they scanned everything around them. Occasionally they'd glance behind, and she hoped they looked like just another couple walking their dog. Cromwell's body language was that of a hostage being led to his execution. His guards were impressive pieces who moved like prowling cats. Ophelia assumed they were either former military or working for one of the Russian armed forces.

Why haven't they already extracted the information from Cromwell and disposed of him?

She thought again of returning to the house to search it as they took Cromwell into the community store. Then she stopped and faced Swanson.

'Are dogs allowed in there?'

'Yes, I think so.'

'Come on, then – we're all going shopping.'

She pushed him forward and they entered the store.

Cromwell and his security had disappeared as she glanced over the cheeses and cooked meats in the deli. Behind that, she got a whiff of fried chicken in a pan. Apart from the Coke bottles and chocolate bars, the shelves were stacked with items she didn't recognise. Daisy pawed at her feet as she checked for her targets, watching as Joe went to talk to the guy at the counter. One of the older couples from the clubhouse was browsing through the magazines when Ophelia saw something that grabbed her attention: a rack of science fiction novels and comics.

She went to them, looking at the recent comic book releases and thinking about her collection. She'd started it not long after her twelfth birthday – and her father's death – after discovering a few novels in his things: tattered books with fantastic covers and intriguing titles. Reading them led her to search for more on market stalls and in second-hand shops. That was where she found her first American comics, copies from the 1970s and 1980s with eye-catching artwork and captivating titles like *Ms Marvel*, *Nova*, and *The Defenders*.

She'd use what little money she had purchasing books and comics before taking them home to read while listening to weird music on the radio or her father's CDs: Iggy Pop, Hüsker Dü, Nico, Lou Reed, PJ Harvey and others in his collection. She'd go through the cases, thinking she might find more insight into why he'd taken his life or discover the details from the woman at that nightclub.

However, the books and the comics helped her escape into different worlds and away from her mother's indifference. In these realms of fantasy, she first read about paid killers and assassins, where she discovered that women and girls could be as assertive and violent as any man or boy.

Now, as she stood there dreaming of youth no more,

CONTACT IN RED SQUARE

phelia had cooked pasta, including some for
utt, and they'd eaten, she gagged and tied
left him in the bedroom, ignoring his protests.
Daisy out. The first thing the poodle did was
garden.

wasn't in the house.

anted to take the dog back to the old woman,
ad insisted on keeping it with them. Daisy
or the plan to work. She'd stood over him as
he mutt's owner and sweet-talked her into
ve the dog for the night. She hadn't taken
ng.

ick walk to Cromwell's place. If everything
ia hoped, she should be on the way to her
fore morning. She practised the stages in her
w it would all work out – getting into the
the Russians, and dealing with Cromwell.
emotions during her assignments, but after
n the store, a slight pang of guilt lingered in

Ophelia watched her targets reappear, stepping out from behind a stack of washing powder. The Russians were carrying full shopping baskets as something remarkable happened: Martin Cromwell strode forward.

Then he smiled at her. 'I don't like modern comics. Give me something from the 70s or 80s, and I'll happily while away a few hours in the characters and stories. And they weren't so expensive.'

Ophelia pushed Daisy away with her foot.

'I know what you mean. When I was young, comics were cheap and disposable, the things your mother could buy for you with the change at the bottom of her purse. She didn't mind that you'd read the hell out of it, tear the pages, and leave it on the floor. She didn't mind buying two or three off the spin-rack when you went grocery shopping. Now comics cost more than novels. And come out bi-weekly or weekly, and everything crosses over and reboots every five months. It's no longer disposable entertainment for kids; it's an investment for adults with jobs. That's no way to bring in new readers.'

His grin was genuine, and she guessed it was the first time in an age he'd had a regular conversation with a normal person.

Not that I'm normal.

She glanced at the Russians, seeing the unease in their eyes.

Cromwell picked up a magazine with a character from *Star Wars* on the cover.

'You're right – and I wish we'd get some proper science fiction on TV or in the cinema instead of these kid-friendly shows and movies.' She could sense he was warming to the subject. 'Not that there's anything wrong with aiming for a young audience, but it would be nice to see some grown-up science fiction for once. And I hate the term sci-fi. My dad used to call it Sky-Fy when he ridiculed me for what I liked. Once, after an argument, I accused him of having no imagination; he said I had too much.'

The Russians had taken their baskets to the counter, and she wondered how she could turn this chance encounter into an opportunity to get into the house where they were keeping Cromwell.

Keep him interested.

'Most science fiction fans are really "sci-fi" fans who have only ever watched their science fiction on a TV or cinema screen and wouldn't know proper SF if it shot them in the face with a blaster. So what's the difference between SF and sci-fi, then? If you take the science part out of true science fiction, the fiction should fall apart. But if you take the science out, the superficial futuristic bells and whistles – the spaceships, robots and blasters etc. – and the story still stands up, that's sci-fi.'

He beamed at her. 'You're not a fan of popular science fiction, then?'

She shrugged. '*Star Wars* is a magpie pop-cultural grab bag of Kurosawa, John Ford, King Arthur, Robin Hood, *The Dam Busters* and what have you. *Star Trek* is what Gene Roddenberry called it: *Wagon Train* to the Stars, with a bit of *PT-109*, Horatio Hornblower and *Forbidden Planet* – itself *The Tempest* in space. *Alien* is a haunted house story that meets Agatha Christie's *And Then There Were None*. While, most notorious of all, *Outland* is *High Noon* in space. The ultimate sci-fi.

'Very little actual science fiction has ever made it on to the screen. There's 2001, *Solaris*, both versions, a few low-budget things like *Alphaville* and *Primer*, *RoboCop* and *Terminator* maybe and not much else. Even *Blade Runner* –

which I adore – is sci-fi, no[t]
easily have been escaped l[
ironic considering Philip K[
writers of all.'

She finished talking as[
Cromwell was beaming a[
lightsaber.

'I'm Martin,' he said.

In her excitement, sh[
name was. Before she co[
Cromwell out of the stor[
then at Swanson.

'Okay, Joe. Let's go s[

Daisy ran around t[
targets through the [
glanced over his should[

Don't worry, Marti[n

A[fter O]
the m[
Swanson and[
Then she too[k]
a big shit in th[

At least it[

Joe had w[
but Ophelia h[
was essential f[
he'd phoned t[
letting him ha[
much convinci[

It was a qu[
went as Ophel[
airport hotel be[
mind, seeing h[
house, disabling[
She rarely felt[
their brief chat [
her mind.

He seemed an interesting person, and there aren't many of those around.

She dragged Daisy to the house with her. The lights were on in the living room as she knocked on the door. When nobody opened it after a minute, she hit it again. This time, the curtains twitched in the window. When the door opened, she kicked Daisy inside. Then, as the pooch scrambled past the Russian's thick tree-trunk legs, Ophelia shouted.

'No, Daisy. Come back, you dirty dog.' She had one foot in the doorway as the Russian scowled at her. 'I'm sorry, but the little shitmonster will crap all over your carpet.'

He didn't move, so she pushed her chest into his, looking for the other slab of Eastern European meat. She didn't see him or Cromwell, only smelling what was once pasta coming out of the tiny dog.

The bloke grunted at her. 'Fuck.'

He moved an inch into the house and that was her chance. She stumbled past him and into the arms of Martin Cromwell.

'Oh,' he said as she used her weight to force him on to the stairs. They tumbled down, grabbing each other as they fell. She lay on top of him as the door's guardian stormed after Daisy.

'Well, hello, Martin. I didn't know you lived here.'

She stayed there longer than necessary, ensuring he could smell her perfume and pressing her legs into his.

Cromwell trembled as Ophelia got up and lifted him with her, his face turning crimson.

'It's nice to see you again...'

She could have killed him then, but she needed to know if he'd already passed any Agency secrets to the Russians. Ophelia grabbed Cromwell's hand and pulled him into the living room so his body was between her and the big guy chasing the little dog around the furniture. She still didn't know where the other Russian was. And she couldn't complete her plan until she did.

'Where's your other friend?' she said to Cromwell.

As he struggled to reply, the second guard walked into the room, speaking Russian to his colleague. Ophelia and Cromwell were between them as the first bloke reached down and scooped Daisy into his arms.

This was her chance.

She pushed Cromwell into the bloke without the dog. They crashed into the sofa as she jumped at the first guy, plunging the fork into his throat. It still had pasta sauce on it as he dropped Daisy and clutched at the blood spurting out of him. She retrieved the fork as he grabbed at her, missing as he fell to the floor. Ophelia twisted around, preparing for the other guard, surprised he wasn't there. Cromwell was moaning and rubbing his head, but the second bloke was gone.

Then he hit her in the back.

She collapsed, wanting to bounce up, but his weight kept her down. He spoke to her in Russian as he shoved his knee into her spine. The force pushed Ophelia's face into the carpet, her lips tasting stale beer as she struggled to hold the fork. It slipped from her fingers as oxygen drifted out of her deflated lungs.

Ophelia bit into her top lip as the mutt barked.

The Russian fell from her. She twisted to her side, seeing the pooch hanging onto the big man at his throat. He dragged Daisy from him, tossing the dog away as flesh and blood sprang out of him like water from a leaky tap. He was struggling to get to his feet when Ophelia jumped over and thrust the fork into his eye.

She left it there, peering at the other Russian as his life spurted away. Then, pleased that both men were incapacitated, she went to Daisy, glad to see the dog was okay as it chewed on a piece of human flesh.

'Didn't that pasta fill you up?' Then she smelt the dog shit again and grimaced. 'Your owner must never feed you.'

'What have you done?'

Cromwell was standing opposite Ophelia, pointing a gun at her head.

'I'm here to save you, Martin. You can go home now.'

'Home? Where do you think that is?'

She rubbed at the bruise growing on her back. 'You're English. Aren't you from London?'

He ignored the question. 'Who sent you? Was it the Agency?'

She heard the anger in his voice. 'Did you go with these men willingly, Martin?'

He glanced at the two dead goons at his feet. 'No, of course not. But that doesn't mean I'm happy with your employers either. They forced me into this.'

'Have you given the Russians anything? Did you sell them secrets?'

Cromwell shook his head. 'They kept pressurising me, but I held out.'

Okay, that's good. Now I need to get the weapon from him.

'Everything's fine, Martin, so put the gun down. I won't hurt you.'

He steadied his hand. 'I thought you were nice to me in the store, but it was all a lie, wasn't it? That guff you said about science fiction?'

Ophelia gave him her widest smile. 'No, that was all

genuine. We can talk more about it when you return with me.'

'I'm not going anywhere with you.'

She inched towards him. 'So what do you want?'

He waved the gun at the bodies. 'I want to escape all of this, the secrecy and the lies – and watching innocent people die.'

'Who died?' Only a few more feet and she'd get the weapon from him. 'I'm not from the Agency, Martin. I work for the Americans.'

Sweat dripped from his head. 'The Americans? Are you a CIA agent?'

'Yes,' she lied. 'You have something the Agency doesn't want us to have – isn't that right?'

He nodded. 'Don't you know what it is?'

She lied again. 'Tell me what it is, and I'll leave you alone.'

Cromwell took a deep breath. 'Those you killed, they were taking me out of the country. I told them I had all the information on a hard drive stored in Europe.' He steadied his shaking hand. 'The Agency has been killing CIA agents worldwide for years, making it look like the murders were by America's enemies and not their ally.' He gazed straight at her. 'That's why the Agency sent you here to kill me.'

'That's not true, Martin. I'm only here to help you.' She nodded at the dead Russians. 'I did that for you.'

'I can't trust you.'

Daisy rubbed against Cromwell's leg, distracting him enough for Ophelia to snatch the gun from him. He stumbled back into the wall.

'Tell me where this hard drive is, Martin.'

She didn't care that much since it wasn't part of her remit, but the information could be helpful in the future.

A nervous laugh crawled out of him. 'Why should I? You're going to kill me, anyway.'

Ophelia couldn't argue with that. She moved, knowing the bullet had to go into the side of his head to look like a murder-suicide job. Then, once he was dead, she'd put the pistol in his hand and shoot one of the Russians to get some gun residue on Cromwell's fingers and palm.

She was caressing the trigger when the kid came down the stairs.

'Is it okay to come out now, Daddy?'

Ophelia stared at the girl. She was seven or eight years old, thin as a rake, gripping on to a tired-looking teddy bear.

'I told you to stay upstairs, Sally.' He looked at Ophelia. 'I assume the Agency didn't tell you about this.'

Aware of the dead men on the carpet, Ophelia spoke to the girl.

'Go back to your room, kid.'

Sally gazed at her. 'Are you going to hurt my dad?'

I was. But I guess I can't now. Not unless I intend to kill you as well.

'That's up to your father.' She put the gun into her trousers. 'Do you want to take Sally away and read some comics to her, Martin?'

'You won't hurt us?'

She moved closer to him so his daughter couldn't hear her.

'I don't kill children, so this is your lucky day. As long as you give me what I want.'

'The Agency sent you to kill me?'

'They did. But I don't work for them, and I'm willing to forgo a lot of money if you guarantee a few things.'

'Such as?' he said.

'First, tell me where this hard drive is. I'll need that to prove you're no longer a threat to them.'

Cromwell removed a key from his pocket. 'This is for a locker in a Paris train station. That's where the hard drive is. Even if I give this to you, the Agency will still want me dead.'

'Leave that to me.' She pointed at the Russians. 'Didn't they search you for that?'

'They did, but I hid it somewhere they never looked.'

Ophelia grimaced. 'Okay. Second, you'll need to help me hide these bodies. Someone will find them eventually, but we should be long gone by then.'

'My pleasure. Anything else?'

'Yeah. Promise me you'll tell Sally the difference between science fiction and sci-fi.'

Cromwell went to his daughter and laughed. 'I promise.' He pulled her to him. 'But how will you convince the Agency I'm dead?'

'That's simple, Martin. I'm going to kill you both.'

TWENTY MINUTES LATER, she'd faked the photos of their murders. Once Martin calmed down, Ophelia got him and Sally to lie between the Russians. She hoped it wouldn't traumatise the kid, but it was better than the alternative. Then she'd smeared Russian blood on their necks to look like she'd slit their throats. The images weren't that convincing, but with her word and the Agency getting the key to the locker with the hard drive, she assumed they wouldn't think too much about Martin Cromwell and his daughter.

'You need to go far away and stay out of the public eye

for a very long time – so no internet presence and no posting on social media. Do you understand?'

Cromwell said he did. Then he helped her carry the bodies into the basement and cover the bloodstains in the room with two large carpets.

'What next?' he said.

'You'll drive us out of here now.'

He held Sally's hand. 'Tonight? Sally needs to sleep.'

Ophelia looked at the tiredness on the girl's face.

'She can rest later, Martin. We should go now instead of waiting until the morning.'

'Won't they think it's strange, you being in the car with us?'

She shook her head. 'I'll be in the back with Sally, wiping the tears from my eyes. You'll tell the guards I've had a terrible argument with my new husband, and you're taking me to my parents.'

He glanced at the rugs covering the bloodstains.

'I guess I have no choice.'

'Okay,' she said. 'Let's get to the car. I need you to drive me to Joe Swanson's place first.'

She might be a paid killer, but she couldn't leave her fake husband tied and gagged in that house.

Now, that's something a sociopath would never do.

12   A HARD DAY'S NIGHT

It was easier getting out of Sunnyside than Ophelia had expected. She was sitting in the back next to Sally, sniffling through a bucketful of tears, when they stopped at the gate. Cromwell's explanation to the security that his passenger had just split up with her husband was enough for them to wave the car through. She guessed they didn't care much about who was leaving the place.

The kid was sleeping when Martin spoke. 'Did you kill the man you were staying with?'

'Of course not. We got a quickie divorce, and that was it. I even let him keep the dog.'

Swanson wasn't a witness – he saw nothing.

Cromwell stared at her in the mirror. 'Does he work for the Agency as well?'

She laughed. 'Joe? No. Why do you ask that?'

The car sped towards Miami airport. With the journey and the time adjustment, she should arrive in the UK around 10 pm local time. She'd reserved a hotel room at Manchester airport.

'So you forced him to work with you?'

'Well, Daisy was more helpful, but I had to coerce him to get me inside Sunnyside and let me stay at his house.'

'So, if you didn't kill him, what's stopping Joe from telling the authorities about you?'

She shrugged. 'Nothing, I guess, apart from me saying I'd come back and wipe out his brother and his family.'

He narrowed his eyes. 'Yeah, that would do it.'

It was the last they spoke until they reached the airport.

'Remember what I said – you must keep a low profile for the rest of your life.' She glanced at Sally as the kid wiped the sleep from her eyes. 'Do you understand that?'

He nodded, and she left them.

'One last thing,' he shouted at her. 'What if I lied about that key?'

She turned to him. 'Then I'll find you again, Martin. And we'll have a nice long talk about dystopian futures in science fiction.'

He didn't reply, and she entered the airport. She felt the key in her pocket, next to the tattered paperback she'd taken from Cromwell's house after they'd dumped the Russians in the basement. She removed it and stared at the cover art of a planet in the shape of a giant skull with a single ring circling it.

It's been a while since I've read Asimov.

She checked in, looking forward to escaping from this world.

———

OPHELIA HAD READ twenty pages and downed a large glass of wine sixty minutes into the flight. Then, after crunching on a packet of cheese biscuits, she watched the Keanu Reeves *John Wick* movie. It kept her entertained for an hour and forty minutes. She thought it might have prepared her for some rest, but she found it difficult to sleep. Even the extra legroom in the first-class seats didn't help. She removed the headphones, about to return to the book, when the smartly dressed woman sitting next to her spoke.

'I wish I could find somebody like that.'

Ophelia turned to her, peering into crystal blue eyes. 'I suppose all the handsome men are spoken for.'

The woman laughed. 'No, I don't mean it like that. I wish I could find a hitman.'

Ophelia grinned at her, glancing around the plane. 'Let me guess. There's an annoying boyfriend on the scene?'

'I'm Delilah Dunne.' She offered her hand to Ophelia, who shook it. 'Have you heard of me?'

'No. I'm pretty ignorant regarding celebrities.'

Dunne placed her hands on the table.

'I'm not quite a celeb, but well known in the world of gaming apps. Do you know what they are?' Ophelia nodded. 'I formed my own company, Deldorado, ten years ago. We make several multi-million selling apps like *Arena Kill*, *Doodle Draw*, and *Dragon Empire*. You'll probably find at least one on your mobile phone.'

'I guess that's why you travel first class and sip expensive champagne.'

Dunne shook her head. 'Silly me, I never offered you a drink.' When Dunne waved at the flight attendant, Ophelia was about to protest and say she hadn't hinted at that. 'Will you bring another glass for my new friend, please?'

It was early morning and Ophelia knew the bubbles would play havoc with her guts, but she didn't refuse the offer. Instead, the fizz tickled her throat as she spoke.

'So why do you need a hitman?'

Dunne sipped at her drink. 'I've just realised how sexist that is. I guess there must be a hitwoman as well, or hitwomen.' She peered through the glass at Ophelia. 'Or perhaps the realm of paid assassins has gone the way of the rest of the civilised world, and they have gender-neutral names now.'

Ophelia stared at her.

Is this a setup? Whoever tried to kill me in Leeds – is this their doing?

'There is a Hit-Girl, but she's a comic book and movie character,' Ophelia said. 'She's about twelve years old.'

'Wow. That's young. Still, I guess it's the best disguise for an assassin, for who would believe a girl could murder people?'

Ophelia scrutinised her face, searching for evidence Dunne knew her true identity.

'So, who do you want dead?'

Dunne frowned. 'I've drunk too much to be talking about this, but it's like that book *Strangers on a Train*.'

'I preferred the movie.'

'You know what I mean, though, right?' Ophelia said she did. 'Not to brag, but I've done so many of these plane journeys, travelling worldwide on business trips, and this is the first time I've ever had an interesting conversation with anybody.'

Ophelia had more champagne. 'Most people are sleeping, I suppose.'

'Yes, I suppose.' She inched closer to Ophelia. 'I did a foolish thing five years ago. Right when Deldorado's sales and shares were going through the roof, I met someone.' She sighed. 'I fell in love, got married, and thought I'd achieved everything I'd ever wanted. That was until a month ago.'

The bubbles sparked Ophelia's brain into action. 'You caught him cheating on you.'

Dunne slumped in her seat. 'Yes, with multiple women. And he's been spending my money on them. A lot of my money. When I confronted him with it, he laughed, said there was nothing I could do and he'd only married me for the money.'

'Get a divorce.'

Dunne's face darkened. 'He won't agree to it and I can't wait years to get rid of him.'

'Killing somebody is an extreme method to get yourself free, even when you're getting someone else to do it.'

'I know, I know. I must be a terrible person.' She finished her champagne. 'If only John Wick were an actual human being.'

She closed her eyes, snoring within seconds. Ophelia removed the glass from her hand, staring at Delilah and putting the whole experience down to coincidence.

Nobody knew I was getting this flight. I only knew a few hours before boarding.

She couldn't sleep and returned to her book.

SHE GOT off the plane behind Dunne, but neither spoke. Because she had no luggage, Ophelia went straight to passport control. She was in her hotel room within half an hour, kicking off her clothes and climbing into bed. This time she slept, her brain racing with images of spaceships, robots and aliens. She didn't mind that; when the dead crawled from the shadows and called her name, she struggled.

Still, she got enough sleep to feel refreshed when she woke

at eight. The shower made it even better, easing the pain in her bones. A quick look in the mirror revealed a shiny purple bruise on her spine as she dressed. She checked her pocket to ensure the key was there before leaving for the train into Manchester. As she waited for it to arrive, she called Katrina.

'I was getting worried about you,' Katrina said.

'How're things in Leeds?'

The line was quiet for ten seconds before the reply.

'I never got there. I'm still in Manchester.'

Ophelia sighed. 'Why?'

'I'm with the Nelsons.'

'Who?'

'The people we met at McDonald's, remember?'

Ophelia saw her train approaching. 'How could I forget? Is their kid doing okay in school?'

'Billy? No, he's still excluded. I don't think they can take much more. Since you know the governors, I thought you might help them.'

It impressed Ophelia how quickly Katrina had settled into the shadow talk.

'Fine. Can you meet me at the same McDonald's in thirty minutes?'

Katrina confirmed that, and they ended the call.

Ophelia put her headphones into her ears and got on the train. When she strode into the fast-food emporium, the music had re-energised her bones, and she felt ready for anything. Then she saw Katrina sitting with the Nelsons. She slid into the booth opposite, peering at the father as barbecue sauce dripped over his chin.

'Did you have a pleasant holiday?' Mrs Nelson said to her.

'Tell me about your son,' Ophelia said. The husband

opened his mouth, but she stopped him. 'I want to hear from her.'

'Billy's fifteen. He spends all his time in the bedroom on the computer or his phone. That's why those people took him away. They said he'd hacked some government computers.'

Ophelia stole a fry from Katrina's food. 'Did they say who he's supposed to have hacked?'

Mrs Nelson shook her head. 'We've been observing that Agency building you went into, waiting to see if they'd bring Billy out, but they haven't.'

'Watching from where?'

'I rented a room across from it,' Katrina said.

Ophelia groaned. 'Why didn't you go back to Leeds?'

'You know why.'

More customers entered as silence settled between the four of them. Then she addressed the distressed parents.

'What do you want from me?'

The mother gazed at her through saucer-shaped eyes.

'Katrina said you know the people holding Billy. Can you find out what's happening for us?'

'Why haven't you been to the police?'

'When they took Billy, they said we'd never see him again if we went to the coppers,' Mr Nelson said.

Ophelia recognised the determination in Katrina's face and knew there was no easy way out of this situation.

'Okay,' she said as she stood. 'I'll see what I can do.'

She exited the McDonald's as it filled up. Katrina left the Nelsons at the table and joined her outside.

'How did it go in America?'

'I completed the job.' She looked into Katrina's eyes. 'I can't promise them anything.'

'I know. All we want is for you to ask about the boy. Will you do that?'

'Of course, but if the Agency and not the police or the regular security services have apprehended him for hacking, it means he's stolen something only a few should know.'

Just like Cromwell in Miami.

'I trust you to find out,' Katrina said.

Ophelia left her, heading for the Agency building and wondering if that trust was deserved.

Moore strode in, placing an envelope on the table. 'How did it go?'

Ophelia showed him the photos on her phone. 'No problems.'

'You killed the daughter?'

'I had no choice. Perhaps if you'd told me about her beforehand, I could have done something different.'

'Traitors hurt their family and the country. Did you find the information he stole from us?'

She placed the key on the table. 'The hard drive is in a locker. I'll tell you where it is when I get what I need.'

He pushed the envelope towards her. 'It's all in there. Your mystery man is Daniel Riley, forty-two years old, with a Liverpool address. After two decades of service, he left the army three years ago.'

Ophelia put the envelope into her jacket. 'I want something else from you.'

'Go on.'

'You need to let the kid leave with me.'

Confusion crept across his face. 'Which kid?'

'Billy Nelson. The Agency took him from his parents and they want him back.' She glanced at the ceiling. 'Give him to me and I'll tell you where the hard drive is.'

His eyes narrowed. 'We don't need to do anything for you, Ophelia. We'll keep you here until we get what we want. You can't leave this building without my say-so.'

She smiled at him. 'Alan, you can torture me all you want, but you know I won't tell you anything. Plus, someone will release all the data on that hard drive to the media if I'm not at a specific place in an hour.'

'You don't have any friends.'

'I'm full of surprises these days.'

He laughed at her. 'Are you planning on retiring soon?'

'What do you mean?'

He put his hands together. 'How long have you been doing this, Ophelia? Ten years? I see the strain on your face. You can't keep killing people as you get into your fifties or sixties, can you? You could work for the Agency full time and not just as a contractor. Then you'd be set for life.'

'You'd give me a pension and a cottage to retire to?'

'Everyone has to plan for the future,' he said. 'Even assassins.'

'Nice try, Alan, but I'll pass. Either let the boy leave with me or prepare for the shitstorm about to engulf you and the Agency.'

He scrutinised the photos on her phone. 'You murdered Cromwell's daughter, Sally, but you want to rescue a teenager you don't know? I find that strange.'

'Her parents are mates of mine.'

'More friends? Something tells me you're lying, Ophelia. Either about Sally or Billy. Or perhaps both.'

She rolled the key between her fingers. 'Why is the Agency bothered about a fifteen-year-old boy?'

He scrutinised her face. 'He stole sensitive data. His age isn't important when he's broken the law and the Official Secrets Act.'

Ophelia moved forward. 'It's connected to Cromwell. The kid discovered the same thing he did. So whatever is on that hard drive is also in Billy's head, right?'

'Do you know what's on the drive?'

She shrugged. 'Does it matter? You can trust me.'

'Trust the woman who's blackmailing me?'

'That's such a dirty word. This is a negotiation, Alan.'

'I can't just hand the boy over to you.'

Ophelia put the phone in her pocket. 'Don't worry. I have the perfect solution to suit all of us.'

She glanced at the ceiling and smiled.

———

THIRTY MINUTES LATER, Ophelia stuffed chicken nuggets into her mouth as she reunited the Nelsons with their son. Mrs Nelson couldn't stop thanking her.

'How did you do it?'

She drank half the Coke before wiping her lips.

'Billy will go to college to continue his computer studies when he leaves school.' The kid gazed at her. 'Not that they'll be able to teach him much. Then he'll go to University. After that, he'll work for the Agency in their cyber department.'

All the Nelsons seemed excited by the idea, especially Billy. Ophelia knew the boy was stuck with the Agency for the rest of his life, but it was the only option to get him out of that building. She finished her food, left the family, and stepped into the Manchester air. Katrina followed her outside.

'Did the Agency tell you Darknight64's name?'

'They did. I'm going to his place now. Why didn't you go to Leeds?'

'I told you. I had to help the Nelsons.'

They took the short walk to the Oxford Road station. Ophelia thought about telling Katrina to stay behind, but she knew this was now the other woman's quest as much as hers. Manchester's rain and gloom settled over them as they boarded the train to Liverpool. When they sat opposite each other, Ophelia returned to the conversation.

'You stayed with the Nelsons while I was away?'

Katrina nodded. 'Apart from their obvious distress about Billy, they were good company.'

'What did you tell them about yourself? And about me?'

'About you, nothing. I told them the bare minimum about me.'

'Did you mention your daughter?'

'Of course.'

Ophelia peered deep into her eyes. 'When was the last time you had a bet?'

'Not since I met you.'

A group of boisterous football supporters were singing in the other carriage, and she did her best to drown out the noise.

'You haven't had the urge to gamble at all?'

Katrina peered at her. 'I've been too busy to think about it.'

'Or it's something else.'

'Such as?'

'We're sixty minutes from Liverpool, so tell me, what does it feel like to be addicted to gambling?'

Katrina frowned. 'I'll give you the short version because

an hour won't be enough for the long one.' She placed both hands on the table between them. 'The first time I went into a casino, I won £500 playing roulette. I was still at university and it helped put a little dent in my debts. Then I started going back a bit more. My studies were traumatic and my parents were stressing me out. Yet, sitting at a slot machine, I didn't have to worry about anything else because the world had vanished. It was as if that was the place I'd been waiting to find all of my life. Have you ever felt like that?'

Ophelia hadn't. 'Nope.'

'Once, I spent twelve hours straight in a casino, my concept of time erased, my body only shifting if I needed the toilet. Which I didn't much since I hardly ate or drank. You keep telling yourself you'll cash out soon before switching to thinking the next bet will be the best.

'And then online gambling took off, first on a computer, then on a mobile phone. So now you don't have to leave the house. Even though the betting companies claim they'll set limits or warn customers if they lose too much – whatever too much means to them – that's all window dressing to those firms. If you drink too much or take too many drugs, your body will force you to stop, but there is no off-limit with gambling. Having no money is irrelevant because you can run up debt until the cows come home.

'So, to answer your question about what it feels like, it's all about the adrenaline rush. It's not about the cash or getting rich because no matter how much you win, you only gamble it away. Gambling gets the blood flowing like nothing else I've ever encountered – it's better than sex, drugs and booze combined.'

'Until now,' Ophelia said.

'Go on then, my new friend, enlighten me.'

'Isn't it obvious? Since your daughter's death, you've become addicted to danger, to risk-taking, and,' she leant in closer to whisper, 'to murder.'

Katrina gazed at her in silence as the train halted at the next stop.

'Is that why you do it, because you're addicted?'

Ophelia settled into her seat. 'I've been doing this for a long time, and the reasons are varied and multilayered. I won't change my lifestyle soon, but what about you? Once this is over, what will you do? Will you go back to your old life?'

'How will we know when this is over?'

'You can leave anytime you want, Katrina.'

'I know, but that man came to my house to kill us. I need to understand why.'

'Did the police discover what we left in those woods?'

'They did, a day after you went abroad. No names were mentioned in the media, but the coppers said it was gang-related.'

'That's good. If the police haven't identified him, we should be the first to search the house.'

'What did the Agency tell you about him?'

Ophelia removed the envelope and opened it. She scanned the details, just what Moore had told her, and placed the contents on the table.

'Darknight64 was Daniel Riley, former military.'

Katrina grabbed the paper. 'I guess they make excellent candidates for assassins.' She smiled at Ophelia. 'Were you in the army?'

Ophelia laughed. 'I'm not one for taking orders.'

Katrina looked at the documents. 'Where do I recognise this address from?'

'Probably because it's near to John Lennon's childhood house.'

'Ah,' Katrina said. 'Brian was a big Beatles fan, but I always preferred the Stones. There was something a bit more dangerous about them.'

'Nothing is stopping you from liking both.'

'I know, but I enjoyed winding Brian up about it.'

Ophelia watched her, wondering if she was as indifferent to her husband's suicide as she claimed. His death made Ophelia think of her father, watching him repeatedly run that knife across his throat.

'When we get there, all we're looking for is information on who hired him to kill me.'

'Sure,' Katrina said. 'Did you check the address online?'

Ophelia said she hadn't, so they searched for the house using their phones.

'I guess he was earning more than me,' Ophelia said when she found photos of the place.

'Yowza,' Katrina said. 'It's a million-pound property, a five-bedroom detached residence set behind six-foot security gates, tennis courts and an indoor swimming pool.' She looked at Ophelia. 'How does this compare to where you live?'

Ophelia peered at the pictures. 'There is no comparison. His clients must have been much more high-end than I've ever had.'

Katrina put her phone on the table. 'If Riley's client is super-wealthy, why do they want you dead?'

'That's the sixty-four million dollar question. Hopefully, we'll get some answers at this place.'

'What if there are people there, perhaps his family? And how will we get beyond the gates?'

Ophelia gave her a brief description of where she'd been in Miami.

'This ain't no Sunnyside, so it shouldn't be a problem if I could get into there.'

'It sounds like I'm not the only one addicted to risk-taking and gambling with their lives.'

Ophelia didn't reply as she waited for the train to arrive at Liverpool Lime Street station. After that, it would be a taxi into Woolton.

Then she might find out who was trying to kill her.

14 THE STORY OF THE BLUES

They waited until dark before scaling the fence, helping each other over at the rear of the house. Ophelia couldn't see any obvious alarms on the outside of the building, but she knew it was risky to go inside without knowing. But she was a risk-taker, after all.

We both are.

At least there were no dogs.

Once over the fence, they crept through the shadows to the back. Ophelia had picked the lock a minute later, stepping into the house and waiting for an alarm to blare. It didn't, and she closed the door behind them.

'Shall we split up?' Katrina whispered.

Ophelia shook her head. 'Let's make sure the place is vacant first.' Everywhere was dark and silent. 'Check upstairs to see if anybody's asleep.'

She glimpsed a shimmering blue light from the swimming pool as they climbed the stairs, stepping off the marble floor and on to a lush carpet. The bedrooms were large and empty, the bathrooms luxurious and unoccupied. They finished in two minutes, meeting at the head of the stairs.

'Nobody's home.'

Ophelia wasn't so sure. 'We'll see downstairs.'

They separated at the bottom, Katrina heading for the dining and living rooms while Ophelia took the rest. Ophelia found no life in the study, gym, or swimming pool. She moved past the flickering water to peer through the window on to the patio and garden.

Is this how the successful assassin lives?

It reminded her of the family home and what she'd left behind. She wondered if this house had ever seen blood staining its floors. And then a long-forgotten memory returned to her.

When my mother found me sitting in his blood, she smiled. At him, and then at me.

How had she forgotten that?

And why had it come back now?

Katrina's voice broke her reverie before she could answer either question.

'Ophelia. I need you here.'

She ran, recognising the tension in the words. When she stepped into the living room, she saw why. Katrina was sitting on a sofa next to a man who, from his appearance, could only have been Daniel Riley's younger brother. He had one arm around Katrina's shoulder while pointing a gun at her face.

'You two must be the Leeds contingent,' he said.

Ophelia held up her hands. 'Look, mister, we're sorry we broke in. We just picked the most expensive-looking house on the street. It's nothing personal.'

Riley stroked Katrina's hair. 'You're burglars, that's it?'

Smiling at him irritated the sides of her mouth. 'Well, it's better than the alternative, you know?'

He returned her smile. 'Sit down before I hurt your friend.'

Ophelia slumped onto the sofa opposite, her mind working overtime. There were papers and a pen next to her, but she ignored them, focusing on that gun.

'Look,' she said, 'if you just want a bit of fun, I'm sure we can come to an arrangement.'

'I know she's called Katrina Johnson, but what's your name?'

Johnson? It was the first time Ophelia had heard that.

'Really, mister, I think you've got us mixed up with somebody else.'

He shook his head. 'How does someone as stupid as you kill people for a living? It can't be this dumb girl act, surely?' He nodded at the papers next to her. 'Read those.'

They were articles printed from the *Yorkshire Evening Post*, all about the deaths of Katrina's husband and daughter – with a big picture of Katrina in every one of them.

Ophelia skimmed through them as she spoke. 'That's not a flattering photo, Katrina.'

Unsurprisingly, her new friend didn't reply, considering she had a gun pressed against her cheek.

'That must make you the assassin,' he said. 'Though I'm having a hard time believing it from looking at you.'

She picked at her teeth. 'Don't worry; you're not the first to make that mistake.'

'Where's my brother?'

'Who?'

'Daniel Riley. I'm Greg. We've worked as a team since leaving the army. When I watched you two break into the house, I thought you were a team, but it's obvious you're not. Did you murder the bloke who killed her daughter, and she saw you do it?'

'Something like that,' Ophelia said.

He laughed at her. 'Man, how messed up is that? You're supposed to kill witnesses, not adopt them like puppies.'

She couldn't argue with that. 'Maybe you could do it for me and I'll be on my way.'

'What happened to Daniel?'

'What was the deal with you two and Duff?' she said. 'And how can you afford this place?'

Riley continued to stroke Katrina's hair.

'We didn't leave the army to work for peanuts. Daniel and I spent most of our adult lives killing people for free, which had to change. Once we decided to do it for money, it would only be big bucks getting our services. So we don't take a contract for less than a million a hit.'

Ophelia whistled. 'Somebody paid you a million pounds to kill me?'

'That's what I said.'

'Who?'

He laughed. 'Even if I knew, why would I tell you?'

'Think of it as a last request?' She kept a careful eye on Katrina's face, seeing no fear. 'So you both worked under the name Darknight64?' He nodded. 'And the contract was through Hitsville?'

Riley shook his head. 'No. The client wired a million to one of our offshore accounts and posted the details to us.'

This wasn't making any sense to her. 'How would they have those account details?'

'I don't answer to you. Now tell me where my brother is.'

'Let me get this straight. The client didn't hire you through Hitsville, and they told you to wait and see who killed Duff, and then kill them?'

'That's about it.'

'But what if you'd got the wrong person?'

'We wouldn't have. The client described you. We knew it wasn't a two-person job, which was good because we had another contract to complete. So Daniel would go to Leeds while I was earning a million in London, rubbing out some rich computer app developer whose husband doesn't want a divorce. I should be there now, but I knew something was up when Daniel didn't reply to my messages. And imagine my surprise when I return home to find you breaking into my house.'

'Are you talking about Delilah Dunne?' Ophelia said.

Riley narrowed his eyes. 'How do you know that?'

She didn't tell him about her chance meeting on the plane with Dunne.

Was it chance or something else?

'The client who hired you to kill me is double-crossing you. I'm supposed to wipe out whoever kills Dunne.'

He loosened his arm around Katrina, moving the gun from her face.

'That doesn't make any sense.'

'That's what your brother said just before he died an agonising death.'

'What?'

Ophelia leant forward. 'And the funniest thing was, it wasn't even me who killed him. When I go, it has to be a fellow professional who does the honours, but to be murdered by an amateur is embarrassing.' She gazed at her friend. 'Isn't that right, Katrina?'

Three things happened then.

First, Ophelia twisted her body to the side. Second, Riley fired at her. And third, but a microsecond before the other two, Katrina jerked her head into Riley's neck. Then she opened her mouth and bit hard. As she did so, it knocked his aim off, so the bullet only grazed Ophelia's ear and hit the wall behind her.

Then Katrina pulled back, tearing flesh and blood from his throat. As he screamed, Ophelia leapt, grabbing the pen from the papers as she went. She landed on his chest; her legs shoved up against his ribs as she stabbed his eye. He howled as she dragged the pen out, his eyeball sounding like a popped balloon. Then she jabbed it into the other eye. He dropped the weapon, his arms flailing as he pushed her off. She bounced across the table and returned to the sofa. He clutched at his eyes and then his neck before falling forward.

She jumped up and looked at Katrina.

'He's after the gun,' Katrina said.

Ophelia watched him, blind and seeping blood, as he scrambled to find the pistol.

And then he did.

He shot wildly around the room as Katrina pushed Ophelia to the floor. They rolled behind the sofa as the bullets hit the walls.

'This is taking too long,' Ophelia said.

She crawled across the carpet, glancing up to see Riley stumbling into the furniture, the gun trembling in one hand while he used the other to stop the bleeding from his eyes. She stood, grabbing an ornament from the shelf next to her. Then she crept behind him and hit him over the head. It took three goes before he fell. His blood covered her fingers, and she realised she'd killed him with a porcelain figure of Winston Churchill. She saw Katrina sitting on the sofa, rubbing her head as she looked up.

'He stank so much I had to stop myself from gagging.'

Ophelia wiped her prints from the figurine and replaced it on the shelf.

'You did a good job.'

Katrina spoke through bloodied teeth. 'Yeah, not bad for an amateur. Do you want to search the house for the name of who hired him and his brother to kill you?'

Ophelia stared at the bullet holes in the wall. 'No. Somebody is bound to have called the police after all that noise.' She retrieved the pen from the floor and cleaned it on her top. 'We need to go.'

Katrina got up and spat bits of red skin onto the body.

Then they left the way they'd come in, cleaning away as many traces of themselves as possible. They were heading out of the street and into the shadows when Ophelia spoke again.

'I hope your dentist doesn't have an imprint of your bite on record.'

'Why?' Katrina said.

'Well, if the police ever question you over this, you've just left your teeth marks on his neck.'

Katrina picked something from her mouth. 'I think there are still bits of him clinging to me.'

They were a mile from the crime scene when Ophelia stopped. She checked them both over from top to bottom.

'I guess we're presentable.'

'So, where to next?' Katrina said. 'Back to Manchester?'

Ophelia leaned against a wall, the cold of the brick sending chills through her.

'No. I don't know who hired those two to kill me, but I've got another errand to do first.'

'Is it strange for Hitsville assassins to get contracts outside the dark web?'

'It's never happened to me,' Ophelia said. 'But I guess it's always possible. Still, what he said was unusual. The client would know Riley's bank account if they'd used it before, but there's something more puzzling about this.'

'How did they know the brothers' address?'

'There's that as well, but I was more concerned about something else.'

'What?'

Ophelia moved off the wall. 'Riley said the client described me to them.' She looked at Katrina. 'Which means they know who I am.'

'Haven't you always thought that, anyway? I mean, why would they want to kill you if they didn't know you?'

'That's true. But I assumed somebody wanted revenge because I'd killed a family member or friend. So they wanted retribution against Rossetti.'

'Your Hitsville name?'

'Yes, but it's not that. Whoever wants me dead is after the real me.'

'Remind me why we're going to London.'

Katrina was adding an extra pillow to her bed. Ophelia had booked a twin room at a Liverpool hotel near the train station.

'I need to warn Dunne her husband has put a hit on her.'

'This is the rich woman you met on the plane?' Ophelia nodded. 'How do you know it's the husband? If Riley was telling the truth, I thought all the clients you get through Hitsville are anonymous?'

'They are. But from what Delilah told me, it can only be her husband. And anyway, I need to give her the option.'

'For what?'

Ophelia smiled at her. 'What do you think?'

'You're going to offer your services to her?'

Ophelia got her phone and sat on the bed. 'The one thing I learnt from the younger Riley in that expensive house is that I must up my game.'

'What does that mean?'

'My clients. I need to be earning more money if I want to retire sooner rather than later.'

Katrina crawled into bed. 'Retire? Aren't you young for that?'

Ophelia laughed. 'The life of an assassin is like dog years – we age a lot faster than you normal people.'

'How much will you ask Dunne for?'

'A million should do it.'

Katrina whistled. 'But how are you going to contact her?'

Ophelia showed Katrina her phone. 'She's representing her company at an exhibition in London this weekend.'

Katrina stared at the screen. 'Gaming Expo 22 at the ExCel centre. You'll offer your services to her in the middle of hundreds of people?'

Ophelia shook her head. 'No, you will. Now get some sleep. We're getting the earliest train in the morning.'

———

THEY ARRIVED at Euston at 11 am. Ophelia spent most of the journey explaining the plan to Katrina.

'There will be cameras in the venue, so it'll be better if you relay a message to Dunne for me.'

'Does this mean we're official partners?'

'For now,' Ophelia said. 'And you'll get a percentage if you promise not to gamble the money away.'

'Isn't this whole thing a gamble?'

'Life's a gamble, as the song goes. So, are you in?'

As they stepped into the station, the rumbling sound didn't come from the train, but from Katrina's gut.

'Sure, but I'll need something to eat first. I can't work on an empty stomach.'

'No problem. There are plenty of food places inside the ExCel.'

'You've been there before?'

'A few times for comic conventions.'

Katrina's look of surprise amused Ophelia. She spent all the journey on the Tube, and then the Docklands Light Railway to get across the Thames, telling her partner about her hobby. By the time they reached the venue, Ophelia was also hungry. So they ate pizza and drank Coke while watching people enter the event. Half of them looked like characters from computer games.

'You should have come in a costume to hide from the cameras,' Katrina said.

Ophelia stared at a bunch of kids dressed like *Angry Birds* and dismissed the idea. Instead, she got her phone and called Katrina's number.

'Remember – keep this on so I can hear your conversation with Dunne.'

Katrina answered the call and slipped the mobile into her top pocket.

'I'll see you back here,' she said as she left.

Ophelia watched her go, hearing her breathing through the mobile.

'It's not that full,' Katrina said into the phone.

'Can you see Dunne?'

'Yeah, there's a huge banner advertising Deldorado with a queue waiting to see her. I'm joining it now.'

Ophelia heard the people inside the centre. Those in the queue spoke about several things: who else they'd seen at the expo; the condition of their hotels; what they got up to in the bar last night; and – for the young women in particular – how much they admired Dunne. The mention of the businesswoman's name resurrected the memory of their meeting.

Strangers on a plane.

Then she heard Dunne's voice.

'Do you have something for me to sign?'

'Yes,' Katrina said.

Ophelia pictured her passing the paper to Dunne, then imagined her reading what was on it.

I met you on an aeroplane a few days ago. You said you wanted to meet a specific Keanu Reeves character. Your husband already has. He's hired somebody to do the job you were thinking about. I can help you. You only need to ask, and all your problems will go away.

'Is this a joke?' she heard Dunne say.

'Not for your husband,' Katrina said.

'James and I are deeply in love. Only yesterday, we renewed our marriage vows. So I think you should leave before I call security.'

Ophelia heard a chair being dragged across the floor and assumed Katrina was on her way back.

Five minutes later, they were sitting opposite each other.

'He must have got to her,' Ophelia said.

Katrina dropped sugar into her coffee. 'Are you sure you heard what you thought you did on that plane?'

'I did. Dunne wasn't joking – she wanted her husband dead.'

'Well, he's clearly turned her around since then.'

Ophelia remembered the look in Dunne's eyes when she'd spoken about him.

'After she read the note, did she seem afraid or confused?'

'No, she looked annoyed more than anything else.'

'He's been gaslighting her,' Ophelia said. 'Somehow, he's convinced Delilah that what she knows about him – the cheating and using her money – likely didn't happen or was all her fault.'

'So what do we do now?'

'There's nothing we can do for her – she's made her choice. We should return to Leeds to discover who hired the Riley brothers to kill me.'

Before Katrina could reply, a tall, muscular bloke came and stood behind her.

'You ladies deserve better food than what's on offer here. So my friend and I will show you some real fine dining.'

Ophelia glanced at the other man at her side.

'You two should bugger off while your fingers still work.'

He leant into her. 'Perhaps you should check with your mate first.'

'He's got a knife pushed into my gut,' Katrina said.

Ophelia stared at the bloke. 'You'd stab her in a public place?'

He grinned at her. 'Sure, I've done it before. I'll cut her so deep she'll bleed out before anyone can help her.'

'What's this about?'

'No more small talk,' the man with the knife said. 'Either get up, or she dies. It's your choice.'

Which was no choice at all.

They left the centre with the men. The one with the knife kept it pressed into Katrina all the way outside and to a dark van. The men confiscated their phones before bundling them inside and locking the door. It was empty apart from dust, with a metal divider separating them and the front. Ophelia pushed her back against the side. Katrina didn't appear worried.

'Is this connected to the Riley brothers and whoever wants you dead?'

'It's possible, but how would they know we were here?'

'Perhaps they followed us from Liverpool.'

'I don't think so. It would have been easier for them to abduct us before we got to London. No, I'm guessing this is to do with Delilah Dunne and her husband.'

'Okay. Any plan for when we get out of this van?'

'Only one – kill as many of them as you can.'

TWO HOURS LATER, they stepped into the grounds of a country mansion.

The men forced them inside the building. Ophelia didn't have time to admire the grandeur before being shoved into a large room. Stuffed animal heads covered the walls, peering down upon the dark-haired man standing in front of a lit fireplace. He turned to them, grinning like a vampire and smelling of an ashtray. Next to him stood a laptop on the desk, the screen showing Delilah Dunne at the ExCel centre.

'It's a recording from earlier in the day,' the bloke said. 'I have to ensure my wife is behaving at all times.'

'You're James, the useless husband?' Ophelia said.

His smile disappeared. 'Insulting me, and I don't even know your names.'

The thugs shoved them forward.

'You hired me to kill your wife,' Katrina said.

James Dunne narrowed his eyes at her. 'You're Darknight64? I messaged you through Hitsville. You can keep the hundred grand I paid, but I cancelled the contract.'

'I never got the message,' Katrina said.

Dunne addressed the men behind her. 'Did you search them? Where's the paper she gave Delilah?'

The bigger of the thugs moved forward. 'They didn't have it on them.'

Dunne stepped up to Katrina. 'What did you say to my wife?'

'Haven't you called her?'

'She's not answering her phone. So tell me what you said.'

'I don't deal with the financial details; that's up to my broker.' She nodded at Ophelia.

Dunne peered at Ophelia. 'Why were you talking to Delilah?'

'We gave her the chance to outbid you. We understood she wanted you gone, and divorce is out of the question,' Ophelia said.

He scrutinised her and Katrina as if they were a different species.

'Neither of you look like assassins, but it doesn't matter now.' He went to the desk, pouring himself a vodka. 'I knew she was thinking of getting rid of me. I was too lazy, letting her discover my affairs and embezzlement. So I had to use all my charms to talk her around. It was hard work, but I convinced her to give me another chance. In a few months, I'll get her to sign the controlling interest in the business over to me. Then, with all the new avenues opening up for Deldorado, it will be easy for my dear wife to have an accident when she makes a trip to China or Russia. So, I don't need you or your broker, Darknight64.' He lifted his glass as he spoke to his goons. 'Keep an eye on the assassin, but you can have fun with the other one before disposing of the bodies.'

The men grabbed Katrina, dragging her out of the room.

Another bloke pushed Ophelia after them. They went down a long corridor towards an exit; one man was behind Ophelia, three in front. They focused on Katrina, leaving Ophelia to the thug at the rear. She scrutinised everything around her, searching for a weapon: bare walls stared back at her, and the floor was empty; either side of her was as blank as her ideas.

And then she saw it.

A paperclip on the ground.

Ophelia dropped to her knee, one hand on the wall while the other grabbed the clip. She moved to the side, extending the clip into a sharpened point.

The bloke behind Ophelia grabbed her shoulder. 'Get up.'

She twisted around and thrust the paperclip into his neck with her other hand over his mouth. Ophelia dragged the clip down his throat, pressing it deeply, so her finger went with it. When she pulled it out, his blood was all over her. She left him slumped on the ground and turned to the others. They were unaware of what had happened behind them.

Ophelia sprinted forward. Two men held Katrina while the third strode behind them. She launched herself at him, slamming her shoulder into his spine. He stumbled into the others, taking them down like bowling pins.

She thrust the clip into the ear of the closest bloke, piercing the drum, before pulling it out as Katrina rolled from her captors. One of them reached into his jacket as Ophelia stamped on his arm. His scream shook the dust from the rafters. She lifted her foot and brought it down on his face. There was no more screaming after that. Ophelia turned to the last man, seeing Katrina throttling him. His arms and legs jerked around like a marionette, but he couldn't shake her off. It took him two minutes to die.

She's a natural at this.

Ophelia pinched the goon with the perforated ear in his Adam's apple, leaving him to choke on the floor.

'What now?' Katrina said.

'We could leave, or we could finish the job.'

'You want to make the happy wife a miserable widow?'

Ophelia rubbed the blood from her hands on to the wall.

'She'll thank me for it later.'

They strode down the corridor as the aroma of death hung in the air.

Ophelia checked the rest of the mansion while Katrina watched Dunne. When they'd returned without their guards, he hadn't seemed upset, only nodding when Ophelia had told him he'd need to dig at least four graves.

It took her thirty minutes to confirm nobody else was there, though she only checked the inside, not the grounds. Dunne was sitting behind the desk on her return while Katrina peered at a laptop.

'He didn't argue when I told him to log in to this.'

Ophelia took the computer from her. It didn't take long to discover the evidence he'd stolen millions from his wife's business. Security wasn't his strong point, as she accessed his Hitsville account on the dark web. She went through his details, reading the communication between him and Darknight64 before deleting all traces. She knew if the police cybercrime officers dug deep enough, they'd find those messages, but they couldn't track any of them to the Riley brothers. She also removed any trace of Delilah's video footage at the Excel gaming expo. Before she finished, she checked the photos and videos, unsurprised to discover many examples of his infidelity. Once the police found those and the evidence of embezzlement, she hoped they'd join all the dots together.

She closed the computer as Katrina returned Ophelia's phone to her. Dunne just sat there with his arms crossed.

'It doesn't matter what you did on the laptop,' he said. 'I'll tell the coppers everything about you when they get here.'

Ophelia ignored him and removed a pen and paper from the desk. She handed both to him.

'I'll tell you what to write, and you'll sign it.'

'Now, why would I do that?'

She sat on the desk, the bloodied paperclip in her fingers.

'How long do you think it will take me to scrape your eyes out with this?'

Dunne stared at the blood on the clip. 'You wouldn't.'

She turned to Katrina. 'Hold him down. Otherwise, he'll flail around too much.'

Katrina moved towards him.

'No,' he shouted. 'I'll do it. Just tell me what you want.'

'That's good,' Ophelia said. 'Write this: my darling wife, I'm ashamed of what I've done.'

He did as instructed, his fingers trembling with every word. 'Now what?'

'Watch him,' Ophelia said as she left the room.

She returned, carrying a large kitchen knife. Before he could do anything, she was behind him, grabbing his head as she cut his throat from left to right. His jugular erupted, spurting blood over the pen and paper, but not enough to obscure the words and his signature. She wiped her prints from the blade when he finished squirming and put it in his right hand.

'You knew he was right-handed from watching him write that suicide note?'

Ophelia nodded. 'He was too stupid to realise what was happening.' She peered deep into Katrina's eyes. 'It didn't bother you, seeing me do that?'

Katrina shook her head. 'If you hadn't done it, I would. It's a shame you never got paid for it.'

'Indeed. But you can't have everything.' She held the paperclip up. 'Just be thankful I found this in the corridor, or we might be the ones covered in blood.'

Katrina took the clip from her. 'Can I keep this as a memento?'

Ophelia laughed. 'Sure, but don't start a collection like a serial killer.'

Katrina slipped it into her pocket. 'I won't, but what do we do now? Are you going to tell the wife what happened to her husband?'

'No. I believe his note says it all. We need to return to London.'

'There are cars outside – we could steal one of those.'

'That's too risky. We don't want anything to lead back to us.' She checked her phone. 'According to the map, it's only an hour's walk to the nearest town. We'll get transport into London and stay in an expensive hotel.'

'And after that?'

Ophelia glanced around the mansion. 'We try again to find out who wants me dead.'

IT TOOK two hours to get to London, and booked into a hotel near King's Cross. The first glass of wine didn't hit Ophelia's throat before she was ready for the next. Her whole body ached, and her clothes had a lingering smell of death.

'You seem to have adapted well to a life of intrigue, danger and murder,' she said to Katrina.

'To be fair,' Katrina said, 'with the gambling and debts, there was intrigue and danger in my life before I met you. But the regular dead bodies take getting used to.'

Ophelia cut into her steak and watched the blood slip towards the fries. She observed Katrina eating, still wondering if everything she'd done after their meeting in Duff's place had been a reaction to her daughter's death. Since Katrina had killed the older Riley brother in Leeds, it had been one long continuous adrenalin-fuelled adventure.

I don't think she's had time to grieve properly for Laura.

Katrina must have read her mind.

'I can tell from your eyes you believe I'm on the edge of a nervous breakdown.'

'Aren't you?'

Katrina raised her glass. 'Aren't all women?'

Ophelia drenched her steak in mustard, mixing it with the garlic sauce. Then she chewed on a thin slice, letting the heat warm the back of her throat.

'I guess we're all just one terrible moment from unravelling, regardless of who we are.'

'And you think I've been too busy with all this craziness to deal with Laura's death?'

'Haven't you?'

'Have you ever lost a loved one, Ophelia?'

Ophelia considered the question, waiting for the memories to emerge from the shadowy parts of her mind.

'Yes. And the agony of it never leaves you. There's a saying that time is a great healer, but that's not true. All it does is numb the pain until something resurrects it. The agony becomes worse when a sound, sight, or smell restores that person for you in that instant. Your mind tricks you and you expect them to be there, but they're not. And then all the bad comes crashing back as you remember they're gone and the part you played in that still haunts you.' She peered at Katrina. 'So I understand the pain you feel at Laura's loss will always be with you, but I'm also worried that you're using this new life with me to push all thoughts of your daughter from you.'

Katrina sat in silence; the only sound in the restaurant was somebody whistling behind the bar. Then she spoke.

'I'm living with it on a day-to-day basis. Duff's demise didn't satisfy me, but his death and the others have been a pleasant distraction. You were right before when you said this is my new addiction, but at least I'm doing some good now.' She gazed at Ophelia. 'Aren't I?'

'Definitely.' She didn't want to push it. 'But maybe we should stay in London for a few days' rest before returning to Leeds. Your house can wait for you.'

'There might be a problem since the bank repossessed the property while you were in America.'

'What? Why didn't you tell me?'

Katrina shrugged. 'It seemed a minor issue, considering everything else we were dealing with.'

'What happened to the bag of money I left with you in Manchester?'

Ophelia looked into Katrina's eyes, searching for any sign she'd gambled the cash away while she was in Miami.

'I gave some of it to the Nelsons. They needed it more than I did.'

You think you'll die soon, so the money isn't important to you.

'What did you do with the rest?'

'I donated it to a homeless charity in Manchester.'

Ophelia grabbed her phone. 'How much do you owe on the mortgage?'

'Twenty grand.'

'Give me your bank details.' Katrina did it without protest. 'Okay, I've transferred £25,000 into your account. You ring the bank tomorrow and sort it out. I can't have you destitute as well as everything else.'

Katrina smiled at her. 'I promise I'll pay you back.'

Ophelia shook her head. 'There's no need – we'll call that twenty-five grand a payment for work done since we met.'

Katrina laughed. 'I guess we are partners then.'

Ophelia stuck the fork into her steak. 'More like you're my associate. For now.'

Katrina's phone pinged in her pocket and she stopped eating to look at it.

'Well, this might be interesting.'

Ophelia sipped at the wine. 'Is Delilah Dunne in the news?'

'I don't know. I set up notifications for any word of what happened in Liverpool at Riley's house.'

'And?'

'A cleaner discovered the body and informed the police. There's no mention of the older brother, but – and get this – a neighbour said they'd only been renting the property for a month.'

'Renting? Does it say who the owners are?'

'No, but I can check online.' It took Katrina a minute to find the information. 'An estate agent called Mersey Properties lets the house. We could phone them in the morning and ask about the owner.'

'No. They won't give out the details. We need to get into their computer database. Could you hack into that?'

Katrina laughed. 'I'm an analyst, not a hacker. What about you?'

'I'm an assassin, not a nerd.' She gazed beyond her new partner, watching the young people entering the restaurant. 'But we know someone who is.'

'What? A nerd or a hacker?'

'Both.'

Katrina narrowed her eyes. 'Billy? You're talking about Billy Nelson?'

'Can you think of anyone else?'

'You can't do that, Ophelia. He's only a kid.'

'He's fifteen. I'd killed people at that age. And he owes me a favour.'

Katrina pushed the plate from her, the food half-eaten.

'And what if the Agency finds out?'

'They don't care what he gets up to,' Ophelia said. 'As long as he stays away from government information, it won't bother them.'

'You'll be putting him at risk if he attempts to find who is trying to kill you.'

'He'll be fine. As soon as I discover who put the hit on me, they'll be no danger to anybody ever again. I guarantee you that.'

Katrina puffed out her cheeks. 'I'm not happy about it.'

Ophelia scrutinised her, wondering if Katrina had substituted her concern for the boy for what she used to feel for her daughter.

'I tell you what – we'll ask Billy and his parents if he'll

help me. Then, if any of them refuse, I'll leave it and try something else. How does that sound?'

Katrina's eyes smouldered as she bit into a fingernail.

'Okay. I'll call them now.'

She got up and went outside. Ophelia watched her walk from the hotel with the phone glued to her face. As Katrina made the call, Ophelia thought of the Rileys and the younger one bragging about how much money they'd made from each kill.

But that had been more lies.

Yet, whoever had hired them to kill her had known the Rileys personally. Did the client know where they lived because they owned that house?

She was considering that as Katrina returned.

'It's sorted. I said we'd meet them in Manchester tomorrow.'

Ophelia finished the wine, wondering if she was a step closer to those who wanted her dead.

17 THERE IS A LIGHT THAT NEVER GOES OUT

They arrived in Manchester in the afternoon. Ophelia checked them into a hotel for one night before heading to the Kopper Kettle café for food. Katrina was covering her beans with brown sauce as she spoke.

'Do you have many enemies?'

Ophelia raised her eyebrows. 'Do you mean apart from the friends and relatives of all the people I've killed?'

'No, it's not that. You said it was nothing to do with your Rossetti identity on Hitsville, that it had to be somebody who knows you since they'd given the Riley brothers your description.'

'Speaking of which – has there been anything else about them in the news?'

'No.' Katrina scooped beans into her mouth, chewing as she talked. 'So, what about your enemies?'

'Where do you want to start?' Ophelia sipped at her green tea. 'Perhaps from my first day at school.'

'Why am I not surprised you were trouble from the beginning?'

'It was nothing to do with me. I kept to myself, but once

they found out where I came from, the other kids couldn't stop their jealousy from consuming them. Looking back now, I can hardly blame them when even the teachers gazed at me through green eyes.'

Katrina wiped the sauce from her lips. 'Is this to do with your parents?'

'Yes, my mother in particular. My father was a politician, so that always annoyed some. But my mother successfully defended rich people in court, which led to her – and our family – acquiring wealth the kids at my school could only have dreamed of. Mother had more than enough to send me to private schools, but she believed a state education was best for me. And it probably was, but since I was the only kid living in a million-pound mansion and getting dropped off at the gates in a limo, I suppose it wasn't much of a surprise when most of the other kids didn't take to me.'

'Did you have any friends?'

'Not in primary school. By the time I got to my secondary education, I didn't care anyway, so I kept my distance from everybody and focused on my studies. Then, a year into that, my father took his own life, and I was the talk of the school again. That tragedy put a target on my back, something the bullies readily accepted as a challenge.'

'I can't imagine you putting up with that for long.'

'You're right; I didn't. It only took one moment of violence in front of the other kids for them to give me a wide berth after that.'

'What did you do?'

Ophelia bit into a piece of bacon as Morrissey sang about a light never going out through the café speakers.

'There was a girl three years older than me. It wasn't long after my father's death. This kid – Georgia – took great pleasure reminding me of his suicide every time I saw her.

Not that I needed reminding, but she enjoyed throwing it into my face and taunting me. I did my best to ignore her, but she didn't like that – so she'd jump me from behind and beat me. So again, initially, I let her get on with it, assuming if I didn't fight back, she'd eventually get bored. But she didn't.

'I saw the mania in her eyes as she hit me and understood it would never stop unless I did something. The teachers were useless, and my mother was her usual distant self – even when I was granted the pleasure of her presence, she was always somewhere else in her head. I was an inconvenience to her, nothing more. I knew I couldn't rely on her for help, or anyone else. So I took matters into my own hands.

'The next time Georgia attacked me, I fought back. It was outside the school gates, with her gang and others watching. So I gave them a show. When I'd stopped beating her head into the ground, the surrounding grass was more red than green. After that, she was never quite the same, always a little slower in the uptake. Her parents wanted the police involved, but my mother convinced them otherwise.' She finished her tea. 'I don't know what happened to her, but I guess she and her family would see me as an enemy. I can't see how they could afford to put a contract on me, though.'

'Do you remember her surname?'

'Bishop. Georgia Bishop.'

'And how long ago was this?'

Ophelia smiled at her. 'If you want to know how old I am, you can just ask.'

Katrina narrowed her eyes. 'You're younger than me – I'd say mid-twenties.'

'Do you need a clue?'

'Go on, then.'

'A lightning bolt hit a tree in front of the house when I was born.'

'That's not a clue.'

Ophelia shook her head. 'My father told me it was an omen. My mother probably thought it was a curse. At least to her.' She rubbed at her throat to force a piece of egg down. 'Anyway, back to enemies. Most of the kids kept away from me after the Georgia Bishop incident. I left home at eighteen and haven't returned since.'

'What about boyfriends or girlfriends?'

'What about them?'

'Have you upset any?'

'Probably all of them, but I doubt it would be enough to want me dead.' She touched her cheek. 'Still, having your heart crushed by me might be catastrophic for the emotionally vulnerable.'

Katrina laughed. 'Have you always loved yourself this much?'

'I've had no choice since nobody else seems to have cared about me.'

They sat in silence, the mood having taken a severe turn. Then it was broken by the sound of Katrina's phone receiving a message. She read the gist of it aloud.

'Barry Nelson's mum says to meet at their house once he's home from school.'

'That's not a good idea,' Ophelia said. 'It's possible somebody has been following me all this time, and we don't want to lead them to their place if we can help it.' She checked her watch. 'Tell them to meet us tonight at the Night and Day music venue. There's a band on, and we'll be able to blend in with all the other customers.'

'With a fifteen-year-old boy?'

'C'mon, Katrina; you've seen Billy – he looks at least eighteen.'

'Okay. I'll send her the details.' She did that, and they finished their food. 'What do we do until then?'

'You've heard a little about me, so it's only fair you tell me something about your early life.'

Katrina puffed out her cheeks. 'Our house was the poorest in the area, our neighbourhood the worst in the city. The building was in constant flux, paint peeling off it, so it resembled a leper shedding their skin. Right outside the front door was my father's new car, which had impressed all the neighbours; unfortunately, the brand new part was when he'd bought it thirty years before, and it never moved from that spot in two decades, looking like a rusted dinosaur skeleton. That car was the talking point of the street for many years until one of the new families dragged an old North American canoe to their front door and just left it there. The nearest body of water to us was forty miles away.

'When people asked my father what he did for a living, he always replied: "I'm a musician." In reality, he was a dreamer, his musical talents never getting beyond strumming a guitar at college. Deciding to have his first and only child when he was fifty years old – I'm not sure how much of a say my mother had in this momentous event – was because he wanted me to live the life he never could.

'I spent most of my formative times in the local pub. My mother ran the bingo club, and my father always threatened to get the guitar back out, but all it took was two pints of weak beer before his ambition diminished and his confusion grew. The pub had a formidable reputation, and strangers who accidentally wandered into it regretted it.

'My favourite of the landlords was an avid film buff, and she covered the bar's walls with scandalous looking B-grade movie posters of films I'd never heard of. Occasionally she'd have illegal late-night showings after locking the doors. So once or twice, I hid behind a beer barrel and stared at the screen while flesh-eating zombies ate sharks or big-breasted naked nubiles rolled around on the floor to some cheesy 1970s disco music.

'There was no sense of community where we lived. Even the families distrusted each other, and the phrase "neighbourhood watch" was just a tag for the local perverts. All my earliest memories are of trying to get away from home. There were hundreds of similar dwellings lined up like plastic *Monopoly* houses on a plastic estate, where nobody ever passed Go and most went straight to jail.

'And then my father got a new job at the slaughter-house, the only employment he could find in a derelict town in the centre of an impoverished country. So he'd come home with an aroma of death and decay clinging to him like cheap perfume, refusing to talk about his day, staring at the orphaned guitar standing lonely in the corner of our living room. Finally, six months into our new life, my mother left him for a better one, abandoning me for somebody else's family.'

Katrina paused for breath, and Ophelia peered into her eyes, wondering how long she'd wanted to get all of that off her chest, knowing there would be more Katrina would need to say about Laura.

But not now. Now they needed a distraction.

'Did you inherit your father's love of music?'

Katrina nodded. 'It's one of the few things to make life bearable.'

Ophelia stood. 'That's fantastic because we're in one of the greatest musical cities in the world. So since we have an afternoon to kill, I'll take you on a symphonic tour of the city.'

They stepped outside. 'Are you going to give me a running commentary as we go?'

Ophelia beamed at her. 'Of course. We'll see what used to be The Hacienda and stride across the famous Joy Division Epping Walk Bridge. And there's Salford Lads Club from the Smiths LP cover, plus the Free Trade Hall, where the Sex Pistols invented the modern Manchester music scene. After that, we'll see how much time we have.'

They headed away from the café, with Ophelia still thinking about how many enemies she'd created in her brief life, while in her head, she heard Ian Curtis singing about love tearing him apart.

18 LOST IN MUSIC

When Ophelia left home on her eighteenth birthday, she headed south to Manchester. She knew the city well, gravitating to its more exciting spots as a teenager. Now she'd returned to one of her favourite venues, engulfing herself in the atmosphere of the Night and Day as Katrina brought the Nelsons over.

'I'll get the drinks,' Katrina said as the others sat.

Billy grinned. 'A pint of cider for me.'

'A Coke,' his father said. 'I'll help you with them.'

'All the years I've lived in Manchester, and I've never been here,' Mrs Nelson said.

'Do you like music, Mrs Nelson?'

She touched Ophelia on the arm. 'Please, call me Judy.' She nodded at her husband at the bar. 'And that big oaf is Bob.'

The kid beamed at her. 'Mum and Dad don't get out much, miss.'

He made her sound like a schoolteacher.

'Call me Ophelia, Billy.'

'Don't believe him, Ophelia,' Judy Nelson said. 'Bob and I have been to gigs at the Ritz and the Apollo.' She ruffled her son's hair and he grimaced. 'Billy doesn't know everything about us.' Then her expression turned serious. 'Just like we don't know everything about him.'

'Have the Agency kept in touch with you?'

'They've assigned a liaison officer to us, a lovely woman called Gloria. Do you know her?'

Ophelia shook her head. 'It's a big organisation.' She watched as Billy removed his backpack. 'Make sure you don't tell them anything about meeting me, do you understand?'

Mother and son nodded as Katrina and Billy's father joined them.

'What do you want him to do?' Bob Nelson said.

'I've already explained it to him,' Katrina said.

Ophelia looked at the teenager as he removed a battered laptop from his bag.

'I'm not expecting you to do it now, Billy.'

He shrugged. 'It's easier here as I can mask my IP address behind the free Wi-Fi.' He put the machine on his legs. 'And I'll dump this in the bin when we leave.'

The boy flexed his fingers over the keyboard as his father inched towards Ophelia.

'I want to thank you and apologise at the same time.'

She waved a hand at him. 'There's no need.'

The alcohol increased the redness in his cheeks.

'Yes, there is. We were wrong to threaten you, and Judy and I are sorry about that.' He let out a deep breath. 'Without you, we wouldn't have got our boy back, so we'll always be indebted to you and Katrina.'

Ophelia raised her glass to him as a way of thanks.

Will the kid be okay once the Agency take him fully under their wing?

She watched his fingers dance over the keyboard, seeing the glint in his eyes and the excitement in his face.

He'll be in his element, working full time as a hacker for them. Though I'm not sure how much his parents will get to see him once that happens.

Judy and Bob Nelson beamed at their son, and, not for the first time, Ophelia wondered what her life would have been like if she'd had a different childhood.

'You're nothing without me.'

Those had been her mother's last words before Ophelia had left that life of luxury. Only it wasn't her life or her luxury. Instead, everything they had was down to her mother's successful law firm. Her father's work as a politician had been based on noble ideals, but it hadn't brought them great wealth – that was all her mother's doing.

'My struggle gets you all this,' her mother would say as she dragged her daughter around the mansion and the vast estate.

What normal person would flee from all that wealth?

But she wasn't normal and probably hadn't been even before her father's death.

The lights above them flashed neon red, casting an illumination over her that took Ophelia back to that day and his blood seeping into her skin. Then she glanced beyond the table, staring at the stage and the people dancing. She remembered being in a similar crowd, pushing and pulling between the beating bodies surrounding her. The oppressive heat had drenched her in sweat. The dancers had lifted her in a crescendo of ferocity, sweaty hands and dirty fingers grasping at her legs as they threw her against the ground. The pain had sped through her body, but she hadn't fought against it. Instead, Ophelia had welcomed it into every sinew and bone, letting it wash over her in a desperate attempt for it to cleanse her past. Ophelia had enjoyed the suffering and danger, using it to release everything built up inside her over the years. Only it hadn't cleaned her as much as she'd hoped. The past kept on clinging to her wherever she went. The killings soothed her mind for a time, each murder wiping a memory away. But even that panacea couldn't last forever.

She peered into the red lights and darkness descended upon her vision, transporting her back to a life where physical and emotional pain was daily. Ophelia recalled a sensation of warm red liquid trickling down her skin, her ears ringing as she heard her father's last words to her, ones she'd forgotten for so long.

'It's best if we never grow up.'

The noise in the venue increased, screeching electric guitars pounding inside her skull. She'd wanted to scream when her father had cut his throat, but her tongue had frozen, and all she could do was stare as the blood flowed from him.

Then it was her mother's voice she heard.

'You're nothing without me, and you never will be.'

Ophelia shoved that memory into the shadows, digging her nails into her skin, and a pool of red glistened in the middle of her hand.

Katrina pushed her head next to Ophelia. 'Are you okay?'

Ophelia wiped the blood on her leg and nodded. The Nelsons didn't appear to have noticed anything wrong, chatting away as if they were on a first date.

Maybe we should have met somewhere else.

'I've discovered who owns that house in Liverpool,' Billy said.

He showed the laptop to Katrina, who twisted the screen so Ophelia could see where the trail had led.

'It was purchased in 2019 by JJ Black solicitors.'

Ophelia peered at the name as invisible fingers crawled inside her stomach, ripping out bits of her flesh. She got up without a word, stumbling past Katrina and the Nelsons to force her way outside. Somebody nearby was smoking and the smell invaded her head to smother her brain. She wanted to grab the cigarette and stuff it into her mouth until it burnt away the terrible taste consuming her.

Katrina joined her. 'What's wrong?'

'Tell Billy and his parents thanks from me. We've got what we want, and I know where to go now.'

'Who are JJ Black solicitors?'

The noise increased inside Ophelia's head. 'Julia Jane Black.'

'And who is she to you?'

'My mother.'

THEY SAT in the hotel bar, Ophelia nursing her second double gin and tonic.

'Did the Nelsons get away?'

'I made sure they got a taxi home,' Katrina said. She grabbed her drink and sat. 'Are you going to explain about your mother?'

Ophelia sucked the gin into her mouth. 'There's not much to say – she's always hated me.'

'Enough to have you killed?'

'Apparently so.'

Katrina stared at her. 'Perhaps somebody in that law firm put the contract on you.'

Ophelia bit through the ice and into the side of her mouth, tasting the blood.

'My mother rules her business and her life with an iron fist. Nothing gets done without her say so.'

'I thought you said she'd joined a cult?'

Ophelia washed her blood down with the rest of the gin.

'The last I heard about her, she had, but that was five years ago. She probably convinced them all to drink the Kool-Aid and went back to helping rich people get away with murder.'

'She's defended murderers?'

'Of course, but only the wealthy ones. They are her favourite clients, corrupt politicians and criminal business owners.'

'Okay, but why would she hire the Rileys to kill you?'

'She wants me dead. I should have realised she was behind this from the beginning.'

'But why?'

Ophelia removed an ice cube from the glass and cradled it in her palm. It chilled her skin and melted. She watched it sit there and turn into water, running over her flesh and dripping to the floor.

'I don't know, Katrina. I'll have to go home and ask her.'

'And where's home?'

'A country mansion outside Newcastle. I don't have a key to the door anymore, but that won't be a problem.'

Katrina downed half of her gin and tonic. 'Okay, we'll head there tomorrow.'

Ophelia shook her head. 'No. This is something I have

to do on my own. You need to return to Leeds and sort your house out. Once I've finished my family business, I'll contact you.'

There was nothing else to say. After seven years away, Ophelia would have a conversation with her mother.

19   BARBARISM BEGINS AT HOME

The following day, Ophelia rented a car and drove north. She dropped Katrina in Leeds. There was no more talk of JJ Black.

JJ Black.

Julia Jane Black.

My mother.

I'd wanted to forget her, remove her name from my mind.

There was a power in names. When her mother had deemed her daughter worthy of her attention, she'd used her name like a dagger thrust into Ophelia's heart. That's why she'd changed it as soon as she'd left home, casting off the label her mother had given her to become Ophelia. And in the world of assassins and contract killings, she was reborn as Rossetti, leaving everything of her previous life behind.

Yet here she was, driving through the countryside to the Black mansion.

Black. It was her mother's name, not her father's. When they were married, Julia Jane refused to take his name, and they didn't mention it around their daughter.

The grounds appeared ahead. She drove past the river and through the woods, beyond the 12th-century church where she'd hidden from her mother's gaze. A flock of sheep peered at her as she stopped at the security gates that hadn't been there when she'd left seven years before. A heavyset uniformed bloke knocked on the window and she lowered it.

'Do you have an appointment?' he said.

Bird song filled the air as the wind drew leaves across the car.

'I'm here to see my mother.'

He inched back in surprise, reaching into his pocket for a walkie-talkie. She couldn't hear his conversation, but he didn't seem happy as he returned to her.

'You need to go...'

She stopped him in mid-sentence.

'I know the way.'

Ophelia closed the window and drove towards the mansion.

If my mother hired the Riley brothers to kill me, aren't I heading into a trap?

Yet what choice did she have? She had never been one to wait around for things to come to her, especially danger.

She parked the car and got out, the sun warming her face. The mansion loomed over her, twisting Ophelia's brain out of shape as something deep inside screamed at her to turn around and flee. But she ignored it and approached the door.

Should I knock?

She didn't, pushing it open, seeing the plaque on the wall commemorating the building being used as a hospital during the First World War. Her father had recounted how the wounded had arrived in their hundreds.

Patched up and repaired so they could return to the front and die.

On her right was an artefact stolen from the Tomb of Tutankhamun, a small figurine of Anubis, the ancient Egyptian god of the dead.

Cursed. Everything born or brought to this house is cursed.

Even before my father took his life, the dead had surrounded me.

She stepped inside.

Maybe my mother isn't even here.

She stopped as a man approached. 'Follow me,' he said with no further introduction.

Ophelia did, staring at the paintings on the wall: a cast of men and women who'd been hanged, drawn, and quartered during the reign of the Tudors. She guessed it was another reason her mother had bought the mansion, to enjoy the daily reminder of how others had suffered for their beliefs.

She entered the drawing room as the man left and closed the door. A rug covered the floor, the ceiling fifty feet above her. Ophelia had spent much of her childhood in this place, but she had only one memory of it. She strode to the spot where she'd sat in his blood, expecting to meet her younger self staring at her bloodied palms.

'If you look hard enough, you can see the stain.' Ophelia didn't move, frozen by her mother's voice. 'Even when he died, I still couldn't get rid of him.'

She took a deep breath and turned. Her mother had eyes like burnt cigarettes, with cheeks transplanted from the moon.

'I'd hoped he'd been haunting you all this time.'

Julia Jane Black walked towards her daughter, mirroring the wolf approaching Red Riding Hood.

'What a terrible thing to say, Anastasia.'

Ophelia gritted her teeth. 'I told you never to call me that.' When she was five years old, her father had told Ophelia her mother believed she was a descendent of the murdered offspring of Czar Nicholas II. 'That's not who I am.'

She was only a few feet from Ophelia.

'Ah, yes – you and the hatred of your name. That's why you ran away to become Ophelia, right?' Her mother's grin made her flesh crawl. 'To reinvent yourself as Rossetti.'

The words shook Ophelia to the core, her legs trembling so she had to lean against a bookcase to stop herself from falling.

'What?'

Julia Jane Black was so close to her daughter that Ophelia saw the sheen of yellow clinging to her mother's skin.

'Rossetti – isn't that what you use when killing people for money?'

Ophelia's legs gave way and she stumbled onto the antique sofa, her hands grasping the plush velvet.

'How do you know this?'

'You always thought you were cleverer than me, didn't you, Anastasia? You never realised how I saw you and him whispering, plotting against me, hiding away to plan all your little schemes.'

'You spied on me?'

'Spying? Anastasia, it's not spying for a mother to watch over her daughter; for a wife to know what her husband is doing.'

'You know nothing about me, and you never did.' *But she knows I'm a killer.* 'Who told you about Rossetti?'

Julia Jane Black loomed over her.

'Why, Anastasia, you did.' Her shadow blocked out the sunlight coming through the window. 'And all it took was a tiny pinch of something. Still, I miss Stella. The meals here have never been the same since she left.'

Stella? The cook!

Revelation pushed down on Ophelia's brain like a meteorite crashing to earth.

'It was you who poisoned me?'

'Can you imagine how many lives I would have saved if you hadn't been rushed off to the hospital?'

'But...'

'Yet, there was the bonus of you leaving your laptop on, so I didn't have to worry about passwords and security. And the things I discovered, Anastasia. I'd always known you were a horrible child from the first time you kicked inside me. I'd wanted an abortion, but he found some backbone and stopped me for once. This means your father is to blame for your crimes as much as you are.'

The memories came flooding back to Ophelia. She'd already planned to leave, had organised somewhere to live, and had created her Rossetti profile on Hitsville.

That's what I was looking at when I took ill.

Because she poisoned me.

'You've known all this time?'

'Of your murder business? Of course. I don't suppose many mothers would believe their teenage daughter could kill people for money, but I knew you could. I'd always known.' She reached down to Ophelia and touched her skin. 'I think this is why I've always hated you, Anastasia, because we're so much alike.'

Ophelia wriggled from her touch.

'No, I'm nothing like you.' She jumped from the sofa and stumbled into the bookcase. 'Did you hire me to murder Larry Duff?'

Julia Jane Black smiled at her daughter. 'I'd occasionally log into that Hitsville site, but I didn't know what you were doing. Then circumstances forced my hand. So I hired you to kill Duff, and then paid those brothers to follow you from his house and deal with you.' She shook her head. 'I would have expected two former soldiers to be competent enough to kill a young woman.'

'But you didn't hire them through Hitsville?'

'No, I knew the older Riley because my law firm handled a lawsuit brought against him by the family of an Iraqi he had killed while stationed there.'

'And you got him off?'

'Of course, Anastasia – I've never lost a case.'

Ophelia's lips shook. 'You go on about me killing people, but how many criminals have you aided to escape justice?'

'You're still so naïve, daughter. We're all guilty of something. For you, it's believing that what you do – what you are – is any different from me and my life.' She moved towards Ophelia. 'You've spent all your life criticising me for not caring about others, yet you're exactly the same.'

'You can keep repeating the same lie, Julia Jane, but it won't make it true.'

'Julia Jane?' She laughed. 'You can't call me Mother?'

'You're not even human, so I'm nothing like you.'

'Of course. You care so much, you kill strangers for money. Duff deserved to die, but of all the others you've murdered in the last seven years, how many were innocent people who left loved ones behind to grieve for them?'

'It began before I left here.'

Her mother narrowed her eyebrows. 'You started killing when you lived here?'

Ophelia didn't want a discussion with her. She just needed to leave.

'Why now, Mother?' She'd said the word. 'Why put a hit on me now, after all this time?'

Julia Jane held out her hands. 'Can't you tell by looking at me, Anastasia?'

Ophelia examined her mother's trembling fingers. 'You're dying.'

Her mother lowered her hands and placed them on her stomach.

'The doctors inform me I have more cancerous cells than normal ones. You might say they've always been inside me, and only now are they coming to fruition. So I'm about to give birth to death for the second time in my life.' She stepped closer to her daughter. 'It's ironic that as I reach the most successful point of my professional career, fate will snatch it all from me.'

Ophelia laughed at her. 'All this because you don't want me to inherit your wealth?'

'Don't be stupid, Anastasia – this isn't about money.'

'Then what?'

'Isn't it obvious? I can't have you outliving me.' An icy breath slipped out of Julia Jane Black's mouth. 'And because I hate you more than life itself. I should have killed you in my belly with that coat hanger.'

Ophelia grabbed a candlestick from the fireplace, gripping it in her shaking fingers, finally understanding why she'd become an assassin.

It was to prepare me for this.

She lifted her arm as her mother grinned at her.

And then Ophelia realised what was happening.

'You want me to kill you. That's what this has all been about, isn't it?'

Julia Jane Black crept towards her daughter.

'You've always wanted this, Anastasia.' Her lipstick glistened under the lights. 'And now you can have it.'

Ophelia peered into the abyss and saw the darkness gazing back at her. She dropped the candlestick to the floor.

'No, Mother. I don't take orders from you anymore.'

Julia Jane grasped for Ophelia, who moved to the side as her mother stumbled past her.

'You ungrateful child. No wonder your father killed himself to get away from you.'

Ophelia ignored the taunt. 'Was it only the Rileys, or have you paid for others to kill me?'

Her mother laughed. 'That's the beauty of their failing. You'll never know if anybody is coming for you even after I'm gone. I'll always be with you, daughter, even in death. You'll never lose me.'

Ophelia peered at the woman who hadn't been a mother to her.

'You can't lose what you never had, Julia Jane.'

She stepped into the corridor, expecting somebody to attack her.

But it was empty.

'You'll never lose me, Anastasia.'

Her mother's voice followed her out of the mansion. She stumbled past the artefacts of death and got into the car.

Then she drove away and never looked back, unsure where to go next.

And then she knew.

She had a friend waiting for her in Leeds.

THANK YOU!

Thank you, dear reader for purchasing this book.

If you enjoyed reading about Ophelia Red she first appeared in the novel, The Final Girl.

The Astrid Snow series
Book one: Don't Fear the Reaper
Book two: The Killing Moon
Book three: Lost in America
Book four: Gone to Texas
Book five: The Final Girl

Short Stories
Call Me: An Astrid Snow Short Story
Dark Snow: An Astrid Snow Short Story

Many thanks to my wonderful wife for all her support and patience.

Extra special thanks to Karina Gallagher for being a dedicated reader of my work.

Ophelia Red edited by Alison Jack.

Cover design by James, GoOnWrite.com

DON'T FEAR THE REAPER

Ophelia Red first appeared in the Astrid Snow thriller, The Final Girl. Here are the initial two chapters from the first Astrid Snow novel, Don't Fear the Reaper.

SUFFRAGETTE CITY

Astrid was used to people screaming. Like listening to your favourite Bowie song or a snippet of religious chanting, it existed at the back of her head, regardless of where she was. The rhythm would twist and turn, the instrumental howls occasionally dimming for the vocals or tortured words begging for release. She remembered one particular shriek resembling the guitar part in *Ziggy Stardust*. It was a soothing sound which allowed her to focus as eyes widened and blood dripped onto the floor.

But this was different screaming, more disturbing than gasps of fear. This was the cry of kids enjoying themselves, a concept so alien to Astrid, her hand trembled as the mass approached. The thunder of feet hurried past her, childish voices shouting for joy as they headed for the playground, leaving the mothers, sisters, guardians, and nannies in their wake. Astrid kept the phone close to her chest, switching her scrutiny from the green-eyed redheaded vacuous-looking girl on the screen to the crowd of adults trooping after the children. Her fingers gripped onto the neon, nails biting into the plastic. All the lesser lights of her past paled into insignificance compared to what she was about to do. Once she found her target.

She took a swig from the cup of coffee she'd bought on the way into the park. It was putrid and tasted like snake blood and bile, a toxic medicine she'd once sampled in the hidden streets of central Jakarta. The back of her throat shrivelled, and her eyes shrank. Astrid spat the drink onto the floor and followed it with the cup. Her long black hair swung behind her like a mane as a faint, transient, wistful smile lightened her brooding face.

A hint of mint and sweetness hung in the air, and she thought of sipping mojitos on a beach. She gazed at the suffragette statues as she waited, staring at the long body-consuming outfits they wore and comparing them to her red leather jacket, painted-on jeans and white blouse. She'd never understood why people squeezed into clothes which were far too small for them. For Astrid, her attire wasn't just for relaxation; it sent out an invisible signal to the surrounding multitude: usually FUCK OFF, but today she was in a more approachable mood.

Astrid stared into the crowd, squinting to find what she wanted. She'd always found it humorous, making her eyes smaller to see something when she should have been expanding them. It was one of the few peculiarities of her childhood she'd kept; that and the escape maps stored inside her mind.

It didn't take long before she spotted the woman whose image she'd studied on the phone: Colleen Moore, Dublin born and now working in London as a nanny. A cigarette hung from Moore's mouth, failing to hide her pained expression. Astrid had scoured Colleen's social media posts and hacked the government website which stockpiled data on everyone. The nanny was squeaky clean, and that worried her. Everybody had skeletons in their closet, but not this girl. Perhaps Astrid had enough to go around.

The stress lines etched on Colleen's face made her look older than her eighteen years. Astrid tried to remember what she had been like as a teenager, vague recollections of hanging around with the wrong crowd. Her mother scolding her for getting up to things she shouldn't. But she enjoyed getting up to something she shouldn't. Soon she'd be getting up to all kinds of things she shouldn't; as long as she didn't mess up now.

There was no sign of the target. Astrid shoved the phone back into her pocket, an eternity of resolutions, doubts and indecisions forcing her on. Was it the wrong place or time? Had she messed up again? The last time that happened, people suffered.

She peered beyond the group of adults marching towards her until the target appeared, dragged behind the nanny in Colleen Moore's cigarette-free hand. Olivia, a small blonde-haired girl, five years old, struggled to break away from the nanny. All of Astrid's buried hopes rose from their sepulchres at the sight of the child. Alien emotions massed inside Astrid's guts, resembling ice cream in a microwave. A week ago, she'd strangled a serial killer in Glasgow, yet now her fingers trembled at the sight of this kid.

As they strode past, she wanted to stretch out to grab hold of Colleen and tell her to be gentler with the girl. The other hand would stroke the long hair of the niece she hadn't seen before today. Olivia ran to the swings, smiling at Astrid as she did, and it was the greatest feeling in Astrid's life. It made her forget her parents' hatred of her; forget the times she'd left home until the last one stuck; forget three years on the street; forget the boyfriend who'd turned her into a computer hacker; forget the girlfriend who'd broken her heart and her arm. And forget how much her sister hated her.

Have I the heart to take the kid from this nanny, to keep her from Courtney, to keep the girl from him?

She captured Olivia's smile in her mind and returned to it over the next hour, watching the kid play with a casual abandonment which only the innocent possessed. The adults supervising the children were a bundle of stress balls, rolling through the playground to keep their kids from hurting themselves. They bellowed out instructions to calm down, but it would have been easier to ask fire to stop burning than to get the kids to obey. Stars illuminated their eyes, every muscle striving to move, to run, to jump, mouths endlessly chattering, giggling, screaming. It was a childhood Astrid had never had.

She was Olivia's age when she got her first black eye. Her mother told the doctor her daughter had fallen down the stairs, but Astrid had never fallen in her life. She'd been knocked down many times, but had always risen with renewed strength and determination. And her greatest resolution was to forget, but never forgive what her family did to her. But even time couldn't wash some memories away.

Inky clouds erupted across the sky. Most of the adults packed up their offspring and rushed off before the heavens ripped apart. As the first drops of rain fell, only two children and their guardians remained. Olivia was one of them, climbing the slide, and then slipping down it, oblivious to the weather. It didn't appear to bother her or Colleen, who Astrid assumed was in no rush to get back to Olivia's parents. Astrid couldn't blame her: she still bore the scars from the last meeting with Courtney.

You're my older sister. You should have protected me.

It was the last time they were together, the night Astrid fled from home and never returned. It was over fifteen years ago, but the words continued to linger in the shadows of her mind. That was when she knew her sister's laugh hurt her more than their father's fists ever did. Now, she stood in the park and rubbed at her flesh through her jacket. She'd put all of this behind her a long time ago; it would be easy to leave and follow through on the plans she'd spent a year making. And then she remembered her niece.

A great pang gripped her heart. She was worrying about what the future held for Olivia, troubled at the possibility the man who'd ruined Astrid's childhood lurked in the periphery of Olivia's life. A harvest of barren regrets consumed her as the gang emerged from the shadows, heading towards the swings and the other child. He was a dark-haired boy of about Olivia's age. The adult with him, a woman in her mid-twenties, was as observant as Astrid and rushed to get him before the group arrived.

The gang left the darkness, marching towards the middle of the playground. The two at the front strode with a swagger born from years of giving orders and arrogance gleaned from the fawning of acolytes. They sat in the vacated swings while the other four stomped around in an agitated state. Astrid recognised the movements of people desperate for a fix.

'Come here, kid.'

His voice croaked through the dead frog stuck in his throat. Olivia and Colleen were in the playground, plus the six intruders. Astrid stood, glued to the shadows, and moved towards the entrance. She stared at Olivia, her mind a barrage of memories long since submerged into the darkest parts of her brain. She forgot her past, remembered what she did in the present, and considered if she'd be this lonely for the rest of her life.

Astrid focused on the gang and knew what she had to do.

PLAYGROUND TWIST

'Olivia, come to me,' Colleen shouted.

Astrid hid in the gloom, small droplets of rain bouncing off the ground.

The druggie stared at the girl. 'We only want to play.'

His voice was empty as a freshly dug grave, his face constructed from crisscrossing scars and a nose which had gone too many rounds with somebody else's fists. His friends were no better, all hollow eyes, ragged, unwashed hair and filthy clothes. They stank of desperation and anti-life.

She moved her gaze from the grunts towards those who pulled their vagabond strings. The dealers were closer to ordinary humanity, clean clobber and gaudy jewellery hanging off them; apart from the one with the swastikas and white power symbols tattooed on his neck and hands. Astrid touched her skin and admired the shine the new moisturiser gave her. It smelt of fresh peaches. She hoped the swastika man was allergic to peaches.

Olivia ran to Colleen, who scooped the kid up in her arms.

'We won't hurt you,' the intruder said. There was deception buried in the quicksand of his ignorance. Astrid wiped the rain from her cheek.

'Come any closer, and I'll crush your balls,' the nanny yelled and Astrid discovered a new admiration for the Irish girl.

The thug froze. Astrid relaxed as she observed Olivia. Silence engulfed the playground before a raucous laugh startled the birds from the trees. They scattered as she followed the laughter to the neo-Nazi drug dealer, identifying him as the group leader.

'Let them go,' he shouted at the shivering excuse for humanity Colleen had shamed. She turned from him, striding from the playground and towards Astrid, who moved into the last light of the day, cracking her knuckles to attract the nanny's attention.

'Yer shud scarper while dohs scumbags are ere.'

Colleen's accent was so thick, Astrid struggled to get the gist of it. Olivia smiled at the aunt she didn't know, her grin warmer than the sun, no sense of fear anywhere on her face. Being this close to her niece was blissful and confusing, the perplexity of the emotions forcing Astrid to question everything she'd prepared for her new life.

Would I abandon a year's worth of planning for this kid? Is isolation still what I crave?

'Don't worry; they won't be back again.' Astrid returned Olivia's smile with her own.

'Are ye a copper?' the departing nanny said.

'Something like that.'

As the two of them disappeared into the distance, Astrid strode into the playground, focused on the nearest interloper and the cricket bat at his feet. She hated sports. Ever since that day at school when she'd turned up wearing high heels and the teacher made her run around the field in them. The bruises had vanished, but the pain continued.

She stuck in the shadows, inching towards them unnoticed, fixed on the weapon against the slide as the invader bent down. She was behind him with one movement, snatching the bat while he reached for drugs inside his sock. Astrid put her foot on his back and kicked him forward. The force threw him to the ground, splitting his nose against a smiling concrete facsimile of a unicorn. The sound of cracked bone shattered the silence. The other druggies stood entranced while the two dealers remained stationary in their swings. Astrid stepped over the one she'd broken as he rolled around and swore at her. She peered at him.

'Obscenity is the trademark of the ignoramus.' A dark veil covered his eyes. 'You think an ignoramus is a dinosaur, don't you?' She thought about it as confusion consumed his face. 'You know, you're probably not wrong.'

Astrid turned towards the leader in his swing. The two dealers stared at her, dull black eyes peering as if she was an unexpected treat.

'Free hit for the first one to take her down.'

His voice was guttural and abrasive, the words jackbooting from his mouth. The chemical zombies didn't falter and jumped at her as one. Their intoxicated flesh and mushed brains meant their reflexes were no better than five-year-olds trying Zumba for the first time.

Astrid stepped to the side to evade them as they stumbled past her. She swung the bat in an arc, bringing it around to smash the middle thug in the jaw, shattering teeth and bone. She followed through to strike the next one in his cheek, sending him flying into a crazed-looking rocking horse. She turned to see the last thug gazing at her in shock, his mouth wide enough to eat a cricket ball; instead, she jabbed him in the gut with the large end of the bat. His stomach rippled under the force as he crumbled.

They lay broken around her, but the two dealers hadn't moved. Fear possessed the eyes of the smaller one; he was no threat. It was the fascist she had to make an example of.

'There's still time for you to leave here pain free.' She twirled the bat above her head. 'I don't care who you work for or what you do, do it somewhere else.'

She picked a piece of skin from her fingers and dropped it, drawn to the bright green hue of his eyes, the same shade as one of those frogs you licked to get high. She'd tried it once and lost two days of her life. The leader slipped from the seat, his six-foot-four frame looking ridiculous in the child's swing. He had a physique best described as lean, muscular, and honed more on the streets than in the gym. His green eyes glared at her.

'That piece of wood won't help you, puta.'

'No Necesito nada para Tratar Contigo,' she said as she flung the bat behind her. He stepped forward, flexing his impressive arms, so his muscles bulged like Popeye on an overdose of spinach. She imagined cracking his head like an egg.

He didn't make the mistake the others had; no impetuous lunging from him, but short, sharp jabs to get her measure. Astrid moved backwards each time, avoiding the druggies on the ground and luring him to where she wanted to be: in the middle of the playground and surrounded by slides, climbing frames and a rocking horse. There was no space to manoeuvre. He was a big man with long legs who couldn't move well in the area created for little kids.

She dodged his latest jab, his frustration growing with every miss. Her chance came as his leg caught the sharp metal edge of the slide. Astrid moved as he dropped his shoulder, dodging away from his arm and throwing her elbow into his neck. He collapsed on his side, tumbling over the slide, lying face down like a marionette with severed strings. The others scrambled to their feet and abandoned their leader to his fate.

Astrid flexed her fingers. 'There's less in you than meets the eye.'

He muttered something obscene as he pushed up from the cold metal. He followed it with some terrible insult about her parents, which she would have agreed with in different circumstances. Astrid allowed him to stand and flail his fist towards her. She ducked before bringing her foot up and kicking him in the groin. His face collapsed, his eyes, nose and mouth dropping like high-rise flats under demolition before hitting the ground with a crack.

He cried amongst the leaves as the clouds split asunder and the rain spat out a thousand waterfalls. Astrid left the playground, walking past the spot where she first saw Olivia's smile. and headed towards the exit on the far side.

She peered into the trees. Is this what she'd gone there for, to find a childhood she never had? Shadows slipped from the bushes behind her, but she focused on images of Olivia. The surrounding greenery reminded Astrid of their back garden, of her earliest memory, of Courtney's fourth birthday party and the gaggle of kids who turned up to celebrate it. Sunlight streamed everywhere as an ocean of blue overtook the surroundings. A group of older children dressed as Smurfs entered the festivities; it was as if a sapphire sea had swept the green grass into another world.

Then her father approached her, Astrid, all of three years old, and these were the first words she recalled anyone saying to her:

You're incapable of love, so no one will ever love you.

She barely understood what he said at the time, but she knew from his face, from the void in his eyes, what he meant.

You'll never be like your sister. Courtney is everything to us.

Her sister's fancy-dress party was in full swing. He danced over the grass, a coronet of snakes gripping his head. Or did she only dream that part? He drifted from her vision and into the gloom. But he was always there.

Astrid shook the memory from her head. The experience with Olivia had confused the hell out of her. That confusion meant she was oblivious to the people following her from the murk and past the lake. It was only when she approached the exit and two more dark-suited men appeared that she realised her night wasn't over.

———

SOME PEOPLE, weak people, fear death. What they cannot understand is how liberating it is. Think of a lifetime of disappointments and regrets vanishing into the next world. It's the deaths of others which are redemptive. Ironically, my first was like giving birth.

The rhythm of the water held me in its sway. The body floating on the river mesmerised me, how the head peered into the liquid arms waiting for it. The tender cadence of the apple-green reeds matched the movement of my heart as the wind moved the grass from side to side, dancers in nature and observers of death. The hair floated out towards the shore, sleeping on the waves as if her spirit tried to find an anchor to the mortal world. It was an image I kept returning to inside my mind, finding comfort in the aesthetic of death.

The dead sleep with their eyes open; the living walk around with theirs closed. They begged for mercy, but were disappointed. They asked for absolution but received no answers. They searched for salvation, but couldn't find it. Some of them desired to cleanse their sins, but no water was available. It was a new life for me, one which tormented me with panic, creating a fear that gripped me in a vice. Revelations greater than most could comprehend possessed me. The dark and relentless fate I'd envisaged for myself had withered into the ether. A fever of enthusiasm surged through me, heading towards a climax which would only reach fulfilment once she'd suffered at my hands. She had to pay for her sins. The water was too good for her. It was for the others; her iniquities would never wash away. She walked by the lake, and it made me think of the different rivers I'd visited, the hunger growing inside me once more.

I needed to get back to the red water.